TO DIE FOR

"A wild ride through the old west, filled with unforgettable characters and plenty of action. *Payback Is Hell* hits all the marks!
You're going to love Evil Stryker!"

— **JOHN PALISANO,** VICE PRESIDENT OF THE
HORROR WRITERS ASSOCIATION AND BRAM
STOKER AWARD-WINNING AUTHOR OF *NIGHT OF
1,000 BEASTS*

"Payback is Hell operates like a confident, skilled executioner
across its violent Western landscape."

— **DALLAS SONNIER**, PRODUCER OF BONE
TOMAHAWK

ALSO BY WES RAND

Left to Die - Book 1

Cross Cut - Book 2

Payback is Hell - Book 3

To Die For - Book 4

The Christmas Slay - Book 5

Trouble in Tahoe - Book 6

TO DIE FOR

Book IV in the Evil Stryker Series

WES RAND

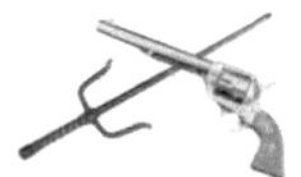

Cover Illustration by Linda Nilsen Worker lindanilsenworker.com

Editor: Stacey Smekofske at EditsByStacey.com

ISBN: Print 978-1-949318-33-3

Digital: 978-1-949318-34-0

For Pamela Mitchell, the best wife and partner a man can have.

CHAPTER ONE

Sitting tall in the saddle of a red roan horse, the man rode out of Pescadero. He'd rested in the small dusty town for the past month, taking morning rides to the northern California coast three miles away. He'd spent the remainder of the day reading and relaxing. Elena, a mixed-breed the same as he, provided beer and rub-downs. The rest had been a much-needed respite.

When standing, he rose to a full height of six-feet-three-inches, carrying a lean two-hundred pounds. A hawk bill of a nose split his hollowed cheeks, concaving under sharp cheekbones. Low protruding brows made the piercing gray eyes appear similar to those of a predatory bird. He had a mustache that drooped from the corners of his mouth, Mexican style, and often a week-old beard grew along the jawline. Long, straight black hair sprouted out from under a dusty, sweat-stained Stetson. A man in his mid-thirties, he had a deeply tanned face with crow's feet radiating from his eyes. They were not laugh lines.

Asian, Mexican, and European blood ran in his veins, making him a mixed-breed. Like a mongrel dog, he never knew his lineage and never cared. He only knew he existed, and one day he would not.

His clothing was worn and used, like the .44 Colt Peacemaker holstered on his hip. He carried a .44-40 Winchester in a scabbard by the roan's withers, and a steel fork-like weapon called a sai, hung in a pouch off his back belt. Previously used as an ancient Asian farming tool, it was converted into an effective defense against the spear and sword. He'd become proficient with its use early on; he was taught by his uncle, an Asian martial arts master. He also kept a straight razor in a back pocket to shave with . . . usually. Once a Major in the United States Army and then a weapons expert for J.P. Morgan, he was on the run for one of the many men he's killed. Tragic and violent losses dogged him. Years ago, he'd murdered the man most responsible for his wife's death; the killing earned him the wanted poster. The other man partially responsible for Leigh's death sat on the roan. Although it had been an accident on his part, guilt compounded the grief. His name, Neville Stryker, was an innocent enough moniker, but time and weather had worn letters off his J.S. Collins saddle skirt. Most folks felt what remained best fit the man–Evil Stryker.

Stryker rode north, heading to San Francisco to meet another man who was rumored to have killed a minor in Park City. That was in the past; George Hearst was a well-respected United States Senator for the state of California. Stryker helped Hearst recover a newspaper won in a poker game, and for that he'd been handsomely rewarded with enough money to live out the rest of his life comfortably. But Stryker could never live life comfortably.

And, there was a woman in San Francisco. He'd see her as well. He'd worked for her before Hearst; he'd helped save her ranch and mine. She'd gotten close, and that was dangerous. All the others who'd gotten close were dead. Jinxed, that's how he figured it. At one time, he thought her dead too. She survived though, and Hearst brought the woman's mining skills to work for him. A damn fine-looking woman. She was the only one since his wife's death to be a threat; a threat to his dead wife's memory–and his freedom. He fights hard against Morgan Bickford. He often put a trail between the roan's ears simply to find out where it led. He told himself there was room for only one on the horse. Stryker had ridden alone since his wife's death.

The second day of riding east on the Pescadero Creek Trail took him meandering up over the ridgeline through stands of redwood, Douglas fir, wax myrtle, tan oak, big leaf maple, and thick ground cover of California bay laurel. Three miles down the winding trail east of the ridgeline, Stryker reined in the roan next to a small running creek and dismounted. Dark came early in the coastal woods, and he'd waited too late to make camp the prior day. Today, he stopped while afternoon sunlight still streaked though the tall trees. After pulling the saddle from the roan and staking the big horse near the stream, he built a cooking fire. Kindling remained constantly damp in the coastal forest, and it took Stryker several minutes to get the little tepee of sticks to start a smoky burn. Gradually, he added larger twigs and then broken branches, shoving them into the flames. The forest lay still with no hint of a breeze, and the smoke stretched upward in a straight column as if seeking to join the big cloud directly overhead. By the time he'd gotten a good cooking fire going, the streams of sunlight had given way to dull shadows. He sat on the saddle drinking coffee, strong and black, and finished the first cup while waiting for a plate of beans and cornbread to heat.

Glancing skyward, he saw the moon peaking around the top branches of a redwood. Stars appeared a little later on, but the canopy of treetops above him blocked most of their show. Tonight wouldn't quite be the same as sleeping under the open skies, but he'd still see some of them as his head rested on the saddle, listening to the chorus of cicadas, owl hoots, and night birds. Occasionally he'd hear a bobcat, or the scream of a vixen fox which sounded like a woman being murdered. The sounds of the woods at night performed for him. At times, he'd just hold the forkful of beans and listen. If he heard a new cry in the night, he'd try to figure out what made it.

How many years had it been, fifteen, seventeen? Shit, he couldn't remember. He sipped on the second cup of coffee. He'd eaten the beans and cornbread; it was good of the woman in Pescadero to fix them for him. *Hell, what year did Leigh die?* Stryker cradled the cup in both hands and tried to recall the year of the artillery demonstration. He finally gave up. He could vividly remember finding her shattered body on the grass, next to the shell crater. Nightmares made sure of that. She'd stayed alive just long enough to say his name. But the day of the week, the month, or even the year she died, had slipped away. He blew out a long breath and let his head dip between his arms. After a few minutes he lifted his face, gazing past the coffee cup and into the fire. *Morgan?* He'd fucked a platoon of women over the years. None of them ever challenged Leigh's memory. In fact, several had died, crossing paths with his life; a life violent and deadly. But this Morgan Bickford woman, she was different. Her mind, what she stood for, the way she faced life, both feet on the ground, fiercely fighting for what she believed. Good looking thing too, and damn, she felt mighty good underneath him. He took a gulp of coffee, staving off the tingling in his groin. Yeah, that woman could make a man forget a lot of things. *But hell*, he thought, *she's not to blame*. She can't help who she is, any more than he could. And he sure wasn't about to change.

He sat the cup on one of the rocks ringing the fire and poked the embers with an oak branch he'd smashed in two with his boot. The embers suddenly flamed up again. He let his mind drift to the next few days ahead. His return to San Francisco would require a bit of planning. What kind of response would he, should he give to Hearst, and what to do about the woman? He absently poked the fire while he gave these matters serious thought.

"Good evening to you, sir."

Stryker snapped up his head. He heard the young man's greeting before he saw him come out of the trees, some thirty feet on the far side of the fire. The skinny kid looked to be just shy of twenty years old. Hard to tell in the dancing firelight. He wore ragged jeans and a heavy woolen shirt with suspenders, no gun that Stryker could see. His face was clean shaven, and no hat covered the unruly shock of blond hair.

"Mind if I join your fire? I been lost all day, and I kinda got the shivers." The youngster waited for an acknowledgement which never came. He tentatively stepped closer and squatted by the other side of the fire, stretching his palms out to warm them.

Stryker stopped stirring the fire, castigating himself for not hearing the boy's approach. Poking around the fire had made enough noise to mask the stealthy footsteps of a stranger. Why were they stealthy? Offering no food or drink to the new guest, he tightened his grip on the stick.

"I came up from our place down off a ways." The young man hooked a thumb over his right shoulder and returned his hands to the fire. "Looking for my dog, he got loose and took off after a . . . fox, I guess. You see'd a dog, have you?"

Stryker'd been studying the kid's face. His gut twitched. He tightened his leg muscles and lifted himself ever so slightly from the kneeling position.

"I'd hoped-" The boy glanced over Stryker's shoulder. The nod was almost imperceptible . . . almost.

Stryker eased to the balls of his feet and sprang across the fire.

The surprised kid looked up at the mixed-breed's body hurtling toward him. He tried to yell, but Stryker jammed the flaming branch in his mouth.

He hit the kid with full force, thrusting the stick between his teeth, driving it down his throat. Stryker's shoulders smashed into his chest. He locked his left arm behind the kid's neck and twisted right, rolling the youngster to the ground on top of him. Stryker pulled the Colt, and fired. The second intruder, older and huskier, had crept up opposite the fire. He'd hoisted a boot-sized rock over his head and looked uncertain as what to do with it. The bullet smacked him hard in the chest. The big .44 slug knocked him off his feet, and he landed on his back with a grunt.

Stryker wedged his elbow tighter around the kid's neck. He pulled down hard, jamming the stick in the dirt and driving the other end still in the kid's mouth deeper in his throat. Stryker felt it bulge out his scrawny neck. The boy coughed, trying to scream. The effort sucked hot embers into his lungs. He struggled mightily, but Stryker held firm. A second inhalation sucked in more embers, and the struggling stopped.

"Donny? Al?" A woman, thin but not quite skinny, wearing a soiled, ragged dress, appeared in the firelight. She saw Al, her older son, on the ground not moving. She looked at him fleetingly and then at her younger son on the other side of the campfire, lying face down. She didn't see Stryker under the boy. "Donny?"

"He's dead." Stryker said, bringing the Peacemaker up again.

"You killed my boys? Both?" She brought a hand to her brow. "Where are you?"

"How many boys you got?" Stryker grunted, deciding if he should shove the kid off.

"Just had the two," she answered, her voice wavering.

"They're dead," Stryker said, now figuring there were just the three of them. The woman, from what he could see, didn't look half bad, but they'd tried to kill him. He had to make a quick decision–fuck her or shoot her.

The .44 round hit her forehead slightly right of center. Stryker pushed off the kid and got to his feet. He stepped around the fire and stared down at the woman. Welts had formed around the black bullet hole. Her mouth and eyes remained open, frozen in death, and she ignored him when he said, "Your lamentations would have ruined the fucking."

CHAPTER TWO

The following morning Stryker rolled out from under the saddle blanket about two miles from where he first made camp the night before. He hadn't built a new campfire, and he saddled the roan without a hot cup of coffee. That caused him to start the new day in a bad mood. He'd smothered his old campfire with dirt and left the three bodies where they lay. He figured it to be close to midnight by the time he saddled the roan, rode two more miles, and pulled off the saddle for a second time that night. Maybe he'd swing down to San Jose, spend the night, and wake up to ham, eggs, biscuits, and finally have a cup of hot coffee. But when he got to the trail junction, he continued on to San Francisco.

Senator George Hearst stayed, or rather lived, in the Palace Hotel on the corner of Market and New Montgomery Street. It was an opulent edifice to William Ralston, who went bankrupt building the seven-hundred and fifty-five room hotel. Regardless, the Palace stood as one of the most luxurious buildings in the world, and the senator, a mining magnate, chose to spend much of his time in the well-stocked bar downstairs conducting business. A man who liberally imbibes throughout the day and into the night while making deals, sometimes has difficulty getting home. If home is a penthouse on the top floor at the hotel, concierge staff can give a wobbly guest a little assistance. However, the senator conducted business with one particular man in his room. That man was Neville Stryker.

An outside observer could reasonably point out that Stryker was nothing more than a hired assassin, a ruthless and efficient killer with gun and blade. He and Hearst got along well. Hearst's last job for Stryker was collecting on a poker debt, a newspaper that Hearst gave to his son, William Randolph, to run. It was a matter of some delicacy for the senator, and a vexing situation. The son wasn't interested in mining; he disdained hard labor. Nevertheless, he expressed a willingness to soil his hands in newspaper ink, and the father would have moved heaven and earth to see his only child succeed at *something*. Stryker collected on the debt. Several men died. The senator had the good sense not to ask questions and expressed his gratitude with a hundred-thousand dollars.

Stryker decided against trying to catch a train into the city. Instead, he continued east until he neared the San Francisco Bay, and then he swung north on the heavily traveled trail between San Jose and San Francisco. He had some thinking to do, and thinking is done better on a horse. Although, he'd come to realize, he couldn't live in the smothering confines of the city, he chose to stay relatively close by in Pescadero. Far enough away to be more than a day's ride, but not so distant as to prevent a return trip if he chose to.

Hearst had another job for him. While resting in the small town, a nagging worry crept in under Stryker's Stetson, usually after the second beer. Was he going to wander aimlessly around the country? He'd originally planned to get enough money so he could settle back in San Francisco, where he was born. However, all his known relatives were dead, and with the Morgan woman there, he figured he might end up in some kind of business. If not a damn dry goods store, or even a seat on the fledging stock exchange, he'd get pushed, or pulled into something where he would wither away and become an old man. *Fuck.* A man who's been in the maw of war, yet somehow lived through it, comes out changed. What had once seemed important, faded away as insignificant compared to living on the razor's edge of death. He'd tried to rejoin civilian life after his stint in an Army uniform, but when tested by his wife's death, he reacted instinctively and killed a man. The courts called it murder. Stryker's code of justice did not always coincide with the law. The bastard stole his life. Stryker took his by driving a sabre through his gut. Regardless, the man who sat straight in the roan's saddle this day, would not, could not, return to a normal life. If Hearst wanted him for a job, it most likely was a task suited for his particular set of skills, and that was fine with him.

A day later, Stryker rode under the arched entryway to the Grand Court's carriage roundabout of the Palace Hotel. The Palace took opulence to a new level. Even the large entryway for a horse and carriage reflected the impeccable assiduity of the designer and architect. The oval-shaped floor with imported inlaid bricks was surrounded by six-foot high urns hosting exotic plants. Above, the open interior towered eight stories, each level adorned with ornate columns. Truly palatial, it had high-tech gadgetry, Parisian restaurants, central lighting, and detailed appointments throughout. Redwood paneled rising rooms, some of the first elevators in the country, spared guests from having to climb stairs. And it was said, most of the West Coast business took place in its luxurious teak and mahogany bar. Stryker never felt more out of place.

The lift operator eyed him suspiciously, but Hearst had instructed months prior when Stryker *facilitated* the Examiner's transfer, the hotel staff was to always allow him immediate access. Besides, the fearsome countenance on the rough looking man who wore a Colt revolver low on his right hip would be challenged only by the foolhardy. Two other men, dapperly dressed in suits and accompanied by attractive women, gave way to Stryker when he stepped on the lift, out of courtesy of course. They noticed with quizzical looks to one another when the newcomer told, or rather ordered, the operator he was to be taken to the top floor which housed the most expensive rooms in the Palace. Stryker ignored them all. The two couples stepped off on the fifth floor.

"Eighth floor, sir." The lift operator opened the gate and stepped aside. He hesitated, holding the gate and door open to see which room Stryker chose. He'd been instructed by hotel management to allow this man access anywhere in the hotel, but that was all he knew.

When Stryker didn't hear the lift moving, he stopped and turned back. The gate and door closed, and he continued down the hall. He came to the Senator's room. The door stood slightly ajar, and Stryker went inside. A small thing, Hearst knew Stryker was coming and left the door cracked open so he wouldn't have to knock, asking permission to enter. Stryker wouldn't ask permission for anything, and with the door like that, Hearst let him know he was welcome to come on in. Downstairs at the front desk, the clerk had told him Hearst's room number and handed him the key for a room reserved for him should he choose to use it. The Senator must have a big favor to ask, Stryker figured.

"Stryker." Hearst stood in the middle of the plain but thoughtfully appointed suite.

"George."

The Senator hinted a smile. "Good to see you again." He extended a hand and two strong grips clasped together. "Let's have a seat, my back's acting up." Hearst pointed at two leather wingback chairs angled toward each other and they both sat. "First, I want to tell you William has taken to the newspaper business like a duck to water. I believe he'll make his mark, and for that I'll be forever grateful to you."

"Got something on your mind." Stryker asked, the question sounding like a statement.

Hearst smiled appreciatively at the no-nonsense man. "Over Bishop Creek way, there's some fellows come up from Los Angeles trying to steal the water. A good friend of mine, Gunner Gaines, needs help; your kind of help. Probably best if no one knows who you are, especially you being a friend of mine." The Senator paused for a comment or some kind of reaction which never came. He went on. "There's a certain woman here, like to see you."

Stryker got to his feet and headed for the door.

"Stryker?" Hearst rose as well.

"All right." Stryker reached for the doorknob.

"You want to know the pay?"

Stryker opened the door and walked out.

He walked down the hall and took the stairs to the seventh floor. After digging the key tagged *"720"* out of his back pocket, he found the door with the same number and unlocked it. Inside, he saw more evidence of the Senator's want of the big favor. His saddlebag had been brought up, and its contents were laid out on the bed. He went to the window. Of course, it faced the bay, and he looked out over the city's shorter buildings to see a picturesque scene of sailing ships in the harbor. Turning back from the window, he decided it was time for a hot bath. Since each room at the Palace had its own bathroom, why the hell not?

He filled the tub with hot water, settled into it, and after sinking down to dunk his head, he began to vigorously lather himself with the soap bar. When the door opened in the next room, he was splashing water on his face to rinse off soap, and didn't hear it. The door closed carefully, making no sound.

"This looks familiar," Morgan said from the bathroom doorway.

Morgan stood erect by the door, appearing authoritative with her suntanned arms folded across full, but firm breasts, and wearing a wry smile on her lips. Her brunette hair, parted on one side European style, hung straight, barely touching the bony shoulders poking through an open collared white shirt, sleeves rolled to the elbows. Her khaki skirt clung to narrow hips at the waist and fell in straight lines to cover the top four inches of dusty brown boots. Morgan's high cheekbones accentuated her lean features and her lively, some would say fiercely, dark eyes.

"You left the door unlocked on purpose," she said.

Stryker cupped another handful of water, using it to slick back his hair. Grasping the sides of the bathtub he pushed himself to his feet. He grabbed a towel off the chair next to the tub and swiped at the dripping islands of soap.

Morgan hesitated before turning away from the door, watching approvingly as he dried himself, then she walked over to a chair by the bed and unbuttoned her shirt. When Stryker emerged from the bathroom with the towel around his waist, Morgan had opened the shirt and was unfastening the skirt.

"Stryker," Morgan began, sounding quite resolute as she looked down at an uncooperative button, "The two times we got together you bossed and tossed me around. Though, I can't say I didn't like it, that won't happen today." The skirt fell to the floor.

Stryker tried not to show his surprise when he saw she had nothing under the skirt or the open shirt, displaying a very fine pair of perky breasts.

"Drop the towel and go lay on the bed." Morgan pushed his shoulders around and gave his back a shove toward the bed. When Stryker stretched out on the bed, hands clasped behind his head, Morgan, still wearing the boots, straddled his thighs. She cupped his testicles with one hand and lightly scrapped her fingernails on the head of his penis with the other. She expected a quick reaction. She got it.

Morgan climbed on wet and ready. "Now take me for a ride."

The woman started slow. For several minutes she just enjoyed the feel of it, rocking gently back and forth, breaking it up on occasion with an equally slow circular grind. She sat upright, arms hanging loosely by her sides, her head erect, and her eyes closed. Stryker simply lay on his back, his own hands resting on Morgan's bent knees, and watched her work. Then she began to add a lifting movement, where she rose up to where just the tip of his penis was still inside her, and he could feel her grip and release on the head of it each time before she slid back down. All made with measured rhythm, her breasts, visible in the open shirt, barely jiggled each time she came down. Eventually, the rise and fall motion took over. The rocking and grinding, although more pronounced, became less frequent. Because she began driving down with increasing vigor, Stryker placed his hands on her hips, helping to guide her as she came down to make sure she didn't bend him the wrong way.

Then Morgan got down to business. She leaned forward, putting her hands on his shoulders; she spread her knees farther out, jamming a swollen clitoris against his pubic mound. But Stryker held her off, pushing her shoulders back, lifting her clitoris off him each time she got close. Finally, when she'd had enough of that, Morgan pulled his hands away from her shoulders and fell forward. Right before she came, she looked straight into the steel-gray eyes and said, "Stryker, you *are* a fucking asshole." It started way down in her belly as a low growl and erupted out her mouth as a long crescendo grunt. She had repeats, her body fixing urgently rigid for several seconds with each one.

After achieving a good measure of satisfaction, Morgan leaned down and whispered close to Stryker's ear. "Now come in me." She didn't have to ask twice.

Afterward, Morgan rolled off to lie beside him. Stryker lay on his back, having decided he liked fucking intelligent women. He was pondering the mining engineer's unique talents when she broke in and said, "I'm kinda hungry."

They chose the Tapestry Room for their dining pleasure. Seated in a booth with curtains, tucked away in a corner, it was ideal for a well-respected man who wished to be discreet. Its Parisian cuisine suited Morgan who ordered veal. Stryker had steak, rare. She drank a delightful Chardonnay from eastern France. He drank ale; he'd built up too much of a thirst to drink straight whiskey.

"Stryker," Morgan began, while they waited for their meals, I want to get something straight between us." Morgan broke into an easy, natural laugh after realizing what else that could imply. A corner of Stryker's mouth twitched. "I mean, our lives, yours and mine," she continued, after swallowing the smile. "I know how you must be torn between the past and present." She purposely skipped mentioning his dead wife's name. "I know how much you like an open trail," referencing his freedom. "Well, I happen to have a past too, and I like my job. Doing my work in mining makes me feel as if I'm carrying on what my husband and I built together. I suppose it's my way of holding on to something we had. I really don't know, actually. I do know I like it though, and I'm drawn to it."

Stryker took a long gulp from his glass of ale and sat it on the table. He figured this was going to be some serious shit.

"I don't want to see you running a dry goods store." Morgan locked eyes with Stryker, empathizing what she just said. "I don't even see you living in the city. It would be like taking a wild stallion and locking it up in a stall."

She detected a slight nod.

"So, what do we do?" She didn't wait for an answer. She had her own. "I want the same from you as I suspect, you want from me. When you finish your business here, ride out on that big roan horse of yours. Go ride those trails, sleep under the stars, do whatever you want, and I do mean whatever. All I ask, all I need-" It almost sounded like a plea. "Is for you to return to me, come back when you can, come here and hold me, and sleep with me."

Her eyes got glassy, and she battled tears. She'd gone deep inside him. He'd never even thought of what she proposed before. If he had, he never would have asked. He had no right. But here was a woman, whom many a man would give his life for, offering herself to him on what she perceived to be his terms. He could have his freedom, hold the memories with his wife without threat, and all she asked of him was to fit her in? *Damn.* He gripped the posts hard under their table. Was he grateful? No. She offered a deal. That's all. He could have his life. She could have hers. *Deal.*

He rocked his head slowly a half inch forward and then back a half inch. "All right."

"Your veal, madam." The waiter with a linen napkin on his sleeve carried two Flow Blue China plates, one in each hand. With an exaggerated flourish, he placed the veal and buttered asparagus in front of Morgan. Turning to Stryker, he made a second presentation, "Your steak sir," and then he spun smartly to leave.

"Shall we?" Morgan picked up the knife and fork.

Stryker cut into the steak. Later, when he asked for the check, he was informed all his meals at the Palace *had been taken care of.*

"He didn't even do that for me," Morgan said with a smile. "But I have a feeling you'll earn it."

"I'll be leaving in the morning." Stryker chose not to tell her where he was going, or why.

Morgan offered another smile, but it appeared fractured. "I have a few inspection trips as well," she gamely countered. "Maybe we can run into each other on your next visit to the city." She scooted sideways along the cushion and rose to her feet. "I hope you have a good trip." With that, Morgan turned and strode smartly out of the dining room, leaving Stryker to finish his ale alone.

Stryker set the glass of ale, still half full, on the table. He signed off on the bill, tossed a silver dollar on it, and walked out through the crowded tables, paying no heed to the strange looks thrown his way.

Even if he wore a suit, he'd look out of place. Some women stole glances of the tall man in western garb. Immediately put off by his fierce countenance, they chose not to make eye contact with the ghostly gray eyes. Uneasy, or perhaps, frightened, they nevertheless watched the back of him walk out with unabashed looks of curiosity.

Upon letting himself back into his room, the perfumed scent of the woman greeted him when he stepped through the door. Not heavy, certainly not overpowering like doves he'd help soil, but it was only a whiff of cologne that wafted in the room. It was as if airily floating on her whisper. Then he spied the scuffing marks of her boots on the bedsheet and unmistakable splotches of blood on his pillow. They were two sets of four small marks about the size of peas, and the two groupings lay spaced about two feet apart. He threw a hand over his right shoulder, feeling for a tender area, and found it. Without checking, he knew he had a matching one on the left side. She must have had good ones, he thought. "Gotta clip her damn nails," he said out loud to himself.

Stryker undressed and settled into the sheets. He inhaled deeply one time, drawing in Morgan's lingering fragrance before allowing his mind to drift into his usual restless slumber.

CHAPTER THREE

Stryker woke before dawn. Morning arrived with stark reality. He took no deep breaths, knowing scented reminders from the night before would have melted into the walls. He opened the window after pulling on his trousers and throwing on a shirt, leaving it untucked. In the alley below, three winos lay curled around a fire barrel, sleeping off a night of hard drinking. The dying fire barely smoldered in the barrel's belly. Stryker figured that was what the end of the line looked like.

Looking out over the city, he doubted he'd be able to tell when the sun actually rose. A heavy fog blanketed the peninsula. Another thing he disliked about San Francisco, the fucking weather. It was summer in the winter and winter in the summer, and it rained ten days a week. People, who say San Francisco is a fun place to live, have never lived here or had any fun. And if he wanted to see any blue sky that raced by the city on the way to some place nice, he had to look straight up. Each new building seemed to grow taller than the last one and they had a way of making a man feel like a rat in a maze. *Got to get the hell out of here and go where a fellow can look straight ahead to see the distant horizon.* He turned away from the window.

Stryker finished his toiletries, completed dressing, and strapped on the gun belt. To hell with the funny looks he got because he wore the Peacemaker on his hip. Few people approached him, and that's the way he liked it. He shouldered his saddle bag and turned the doorknob.

The hotel coachman, wearing a bright red coat with tails and a black top hat, saw Stryker approaching. He raised an arm, signaling a young attendant waiting by the arched entryway, he wanted a horse brought up. "Nineteen!" The boy jumped to his feet and took off out of sight. Stryker walked up to stand beside the coachman who attempted to buy time for the lad by offering pleasantries to his early morning guest. The pleasantries were extended in vain to a man incapable of returning them. The boy and the roan, already saddled, came around the corner and under the archway. Stryker scowled at the coachman.

"We saddle them first thing in the morning, sir. It's taken off after the concierge has ascertained the guest will not be requiring his mount for the day." The coachman doffed his top hat. He perhaps guessed Stryker's annoyance thinking a horse stood saddled all night.

Stryker took the reins and led the roan through the grand court archway and two blocks down Market Street before he mounted up. Few people were out this morning. It was Saturday, and thick fog nesting in the city kept the dark hours hanging around. Those he met simply faded in and out of the mist. He kept the roan at a slow walk until the angular shadow of the ferry house took shape, appearing as a ghostly, hulking structure not quite fifty yards ahead on the Embarcadero. The roan horse stopped in front of the building without Stryker having to tug on the reins. He slid off, pulled the carry bag from around the saddle horn, and handed the reins to the stableman.

"Will you be taking the ferry this morning, sir?"

"The 'eight-ten' to Alameda," Stryker answered, "The horse too."

"Yes sir. Get tickets inside. You'll need to show 'em in Alameda to claim your horse. I'll make sure he's boarded on." The stableman waited for the customary tip, but then after getting a good look at Stryker's stern features, he decided not to push it. He turned and walked away with the roan.

Inside the ferry house, Stryker learned the eight-ten ferry to Alameda was on time; however, the train he planned to take from there to Carson

City was delayed for several hours. After buying a mug of steaming black coffee from a deli worker who hated her job, he made his way across the room, took a stool, and threw the bag on a counter under a row of windows looking out toward Market Street. He had two hours before the ferry left to cross the bay. The coffee tasted strong and hot, the way he liked it, and he held the mug in both hands. San Francisco's cold damp weather invaded a body and chilled the bones like a cold-hearted woman. As he sipped the coffee, Stryker looked around the cavernous station house. Not many other would-be passengers had arrived yet. He could have stayed in bed another hour or so, but he wanted out of the city. He lingered on that a moment and then thought about why he took on another job from Hearst. A worker passed by, pushing a cart stacked high with baggage. The man struggled to keep a straight line with the heavy load, and he weaved his way across the floor to a numbered ramp far down the hall. *Maybe the fellow and I just do what we can do*, he thought. That man pushed a cart. He used a gun. Sometimes he used a blade, he allowed, and he grunted as he sipped from the mug. And the job? Why take it, if he already had enough money to live on? *Well*, he guessed, *it came from some deep need for a sense of purpose*. Sitting around on his ass seemed awfully boring. What else could he do? He knew how to mix steel and blood on the battlefield using artillery, but he'd grown tired of the army and all its authoritarianism. Investment Banking? He'd killed too many men - and women - to be a respected business man. He was a wanted man for more than one murder. He envisioned his introductions to shareholders. "Yes, our corporate officer is a West Point graduate and a cold-blooded killer." That last part kinda blemished the resume. *Well*, he finally reasoned, *we all do what we can do*.

"Them young boys asking for trouble."

Stryker swiveled on the stool to face a haggard old man looking out the window. Nothing stood out about him. Of average height and weight, he could have been fifty-five or sixty-five, hard to tell. His closely cropped hair hid its true color, and his pale, patchy skin showed little sun damage. The blue-gray eyes had the shape of a tired, beaten man. A sadness hung heavy on him. The man could have been talking to himself, but Stryker saw three young ruffians outside the glass menacing an older man dressed in a business suit. The fog remained heavy, and he could barely see the scuffling. One of the boys jumped behind the gentleman and hooked elbows with him, pulling the man's arms rearward. Another boy darted forward, reached inside his coat, and grabbed what appeared to be a wallet. The three thieves took off running and disappeared in the fog.

"I used to be one of them." The old man said into the glass. Then he let out a long breath and turned toward Stryker. "And I spent most of my life in prison."

Stryker brought the cup to his mouth and took a sip without comment.

"Thought I was too smart to work for money." The old man pointed with his thumb. "Just like them dumb shits. Then one night one of us killed a man. Turned out he's a big shot in the state. We got caught, and we got life. The other two died in that damned hole. Somebody had 'em killed, I reckon. And they put me in solitaire to save my life. Twenty-seven years, twenty-seven long, God-damned years alone."

Stryker thought about getting up and leaving, but the station was beginning to fill and he'd rather hear the old man out than stand. He shifted around and watched the incoming crowd.

"You been in prison son?"

Stryker ignored the old man's question.

"Ever kill anybody?"

Same response.

"The war. You in it?"

"Yeah, I was in it." Stryker said, without realizing he'd spoken out loud. He kept gazing at the station's interior without glancing at the old fellow next to him.

"Then you've killed."

At that, Stryker turned.

The steely glare, its icy cruelty, caught the old man by surprise. "I guess they deserved it."

"Most did," Stryker said, issuing a thinly disguised threat.

"Uh, some died . . . maybe shouldn't have?" The old man knew he was in dangerous territory but asked, anyway. "Why d'you kill 'em?"

"Asked too many questions."

"Name's Albert." He cracked a crooked grin and stuck out his hand. He withdrew it when the handshake never came. The smile slunk from his face as if embarrassed it showed itself in the first place. He changed the subject. "When I said one of us killed a man, I didn't do it. I was just stupid enough to be part of it."

Stryker sat down the coffee mug and swung around to watch the crowd grow. He leaned back and rested his elbows on the counter.

"I ain't done much talking the past twenty-some years. Don't mean to wear your ears out." Albert must have taken Stryker not punching him or not walking off as an invitation. He stared out the window, not really focusing on anything. "You don't seem like them boys out there, or me, and . . ." He stopped in mid-sentence. "We was always looking for trouble, dumb fools." He turned away from the glass and to the mixed breed. "I reckon trouble found you and regretted it." After taking a breath of resignation, Albert swung the rest of the way around and mimicked Stryker, putting his elbows on the counter. "I ain't done shit with my life."

Stryker glanced at Albert. Not often a man faces up to the truth about himself. Maybe Albert got to the end, useless to bullshit.

"I had a wife once, a young pretty thing. I told her all these lies about how I was gonna make us a good life. I'd like to say I tried hard to be a good husband for her, but that ain't true. I'd stole what little I gave her, after I drank and gambled the rest away. She begged me to do things right." Albert used his elbows to push away from the counter and sat up. "I thought the way she always said how much she loved me I could get away with anything. She stayed by my side for nine years. For nine years I shit on her. Then, when I went to prison she left. I ain't seen her since. I thought about Mary ever' day for thirty-four years. At first, I figured she left right away. That was 'fore I found out the prison weren't lettin' no one see me. She mighta hung around for some time longer. I don't know. So here I am, a good for nothing, worthless pile of shit. Old shit now." He looked at Stryker. "Where you goin' mister?"

"Bishop Creek," Stryker answered flatly.

"Well, they gave me enough money to get across the bay. Reckon I'll go from there. I'll be seeing you."

"Stryker."

"What you say mister?" Albert had leaned forward to get up, but he hesitated and swiveled his head sideways at Stryker.

"Name's Stryker."

Albert managed a faint smile and slipped from the stool.

Stryker watched the old man limp away.

Stryker plunked the empty mug on the counter and rose to go find the roan. When assured his horse would be boarded on the ferry, he used the wait prior to boarding to walk along the docks. Presently, he queued up by the gate, and shuffled through it, and then onto the ferryboat. Fog had begun to lift its skirts on the San Francisco side of the bay. Halfway to Alameda, it pulled them up entirely. As has become his custom on the ferries, Stryker chose to stay outside and on the upper deck, eschewing the smothering confines below. He kept to himself and spurned conversations with the friendly, or the curious, by simply walking away. Albert, if he were on board, also made himself scarce, because Stryker didn't see him during the entire crossing.

He'd waited three hours in Oakland for the Carson City train. Breakdowns on the narrow-gauge rails became more frequent since train companies started ripping up the rickety rails and replacing them with heavier standard track. Narrow gauge track maintenance suffered.

Two blocks from the train station Stryker stumbled upon a restaurant called Good Eats. It advertised "Momma's Home Cooked Meals" below its name, and he turned the doorknob to go inside. After he got the food, he figured the husband and kids ran off because of Momma's cooking. The steak was gristly and tough, and he picked up the two eggs in one piece and ate them in his hand like a piece of toast. He tried the coffee and planted the cup on the table after one drink. Momma surely made it with mop water. He threw two bits on the table, picked up his bag, and headed out the rear door with "Backhouse" above the doorway.

Two little buildings, one had "Men" in white paint on its door and the other one, also in white paint, had "Gals" scrawled on it. They stood about forty paces out back of Good Eats. *Considerate of Momma to have separate shit houses, and to put them far enough away so the shit smell out here didn't interfere with the shit served inside,* Stryker thought.

As he swung the privy door open, a man's arm reached around the rear corner, and clutched at an uneven board. Stryker shifted the bag to his left hand and draped his hand over the butt of the Peacemaker. Stryker pulled the six-gun and pointed it at the corner. A man staggered into full view and collapsed on the ground. When he rolled over, a pancake sized splotch of blood showed above the belt line on his left side. A darker swath cascaded down his pant leg. Stryker holstered the Colt, set the carry bag down, and knelt by the man he almost didn't recognize because of the ashen face from blood loss.

"Them youngin's stuck me pretty good." Albert coughed and managed to prop himself up on one elbow. "Same boys, ah . . .," he grimaced as he spoke.

"I'll get a doctor."

"No." Albert shook his head. "Just wanted to tell who . . . did it. I ain't fit for livin' outta jail, Stryker," he said, with words trailing off in a whisper. He lifted his eyes to Stryker's. "I'll let it end here next to the shithouse." Albert's arm gave way and he fell onto his back. His breathing became a death rattle.

Stryker felt the carry bag slide against his knee. He spun around. Brownie, the thief, crouched in a sprint, and hugging the bag under an arm, was on the second step of his dash.

Stryker lunged flat out, stretched out an arm, and swatted a boot heel. The boot smacked into the other, sending the tripped runner sprawling in the dirt. Like a cat Stryker was on him. He pulled the razor from his back pocket–and used it.

Two young men waited at the Good Eats back corner. Nat stood with a shovel raised over his head. Butch, gripping a butcher knife, made stabbing moves in the air.

With the energy of a terrified animal Brownie somehow scrambled out from under Stryker. He let go of the bag and struggled to his feet. But, when the foiled thief made it to the corner of the restaurant, his strength flagged. He stumbled around the edge of the building and came face to face with the knife holder.

Brownie grabbed for Butch's shoulders and mimed "Help Me!" The plea morphed into a guttural gurgle. It detoured out the crimson gap in his throat, riding on blood from a severed windpipe. Blood sprayed Butch's face and eyes. He screamed loud, very loud, like a woman in painful childbirth, and shoved Brownie off him, forgetting he still held the knife.

Brownie hardly felt the blade go in as he slid to the ground dying.

The scream drew several people from the street and nearby buildings, including five out of Good Eats, who would not return and pay for their food.

Nat peaked around the corner and only spied Albert lying by the privy. He turned to Butch. "What the hell happened? All I see is that old man, dead!"

"Grab 'em!" Someone yelled from the gathering crowd.

"Drop the knife!" Another man ordered.

Butch let the blade fall to the dirt.

The two young men were arrested and tried. Eventually, Butch was found guilty of two murders and hanged. Nat was sentenced to fifteen years. When he got out of prison, he traveled south to Los Angeles and became a bookkeeper.

Albert never knew his wife Mary was pregnant with his son when she tried to visit him in prison. She finally gave up trying to see him after the boy turned two years old. She traveled east to Virginia and never tried to contact Albert again. Albert's son grew up and stayed in Virginia, becoming a lawyer at the age of twenty-four. There he raised his own family.

Generations later in Washington D.C. a man in the secret service assigned to protect the President of the United States, stepped in front of a bullet intended to kill the President. Albert's blood ran in the agent's veins.

· · ·

Stryker thought it better to save his pee for somewhere else. He picked up his carry bag and made his way up the other alley of the Good Eats restaurant. About halfway to the front street he heard what sounded like a woman's scream. It seemed about time for a beer.

He swung by the train station five blocks away for an updated departure time, and he also made sure the roan had been led over to the holding corral. Then he headed for the nearest saloon. The sign hanging outside said, "Eugene's Cold Beer." After making room for a beer in the *three-holer* behind the saloon, he went inside and ordered a tall glass of brew. In small towns, the beer was served near room temperature. Here, the bartender sat a frosty glass of cold beer on the counter.

"Busch beer," the barkeep said, noting Stryker's curiosity. "First of its kind. You don't like it; I got warm if you want."

Stryker picked up the mug by its handle and took a sip of the frothy liquid. He tried it again, and then carried the glass to an empty table. His first thoughts after sitting on a hard, straight-back chair, was a fellow could come to like this beer. Then his mind drifted to how he was to comport himself when he got to Laws. He wouldn't like it, but he decided to have the Peacemaker in his saddlebag when he arrived in town. Maybe, he thought as he slowly rotated the glass in a puddle of beer, he could get on as a hired hand with the Gaines man. If blood is to be spilled, he ought to find out who should do the spilling. The second beer tasted pretty good too.

Train delays kept coming. Stryker began to think he would have to ride the damn horse to Laws. Finally, around dusk, the Southern Pacific rolled into Oakland. An hour later, Stryker and the roan rode in the train bound for Carson City. Being a typical train coach, it had rows of wooden bench seats on each side of the car. A bench accommodated two fully grown adults, or maybe two women and a child. As was his custom, he took a seat on the last bench facing forward. Military training; it gave him a chance to see who got on without being seen first. Habit. He never gave it much thought, but it was one of those little things which helped keep him out of a grave. Little things can cost a man his life.

Train couplers started their sequential clunking down from the Shay locomotive and the coach began a slow roll when two girls bustled through the front door, wrestling with what seemed like six months' worth of baggage. Although the car was crowded, the bench opposite Stryker remained empty. That bench faced the rear of the coach, and it faced him. Both prospective arrangements must have seemed uninviting. Perhaps Stryker gave the impression he slept, having lowered the Stetson thereby covering his fierce facial features–the ghostly eyes at least–and his long legs stretching across the narrow aisle. Stryker seldom slept, soundly anyway. Years in the army saw to that. No one in the army sleeps *well*. And then there were the memories, haunting memories of guilt and grief. Not of those he killed with purpose, just of the one singular death which never dulled with time. He expected the years to wash away much of what took place the day his wife died. He gave up that happening years ago. He slept about as soundly as he would on a mattress filled with rocks.

Two young ladies struggled down the aisle banging against passengers on their way. The already seated dared not scoot over, thereby opening up a seat. The girls' grunts of frustration made several of the male passengers squirm with indecision, but the men wisely chose not to help girls who were easy on the eyes. Husbands, who embarrassed wives by aiding a pretty girl, endured a living hell for a long fucking time. Eventually, the girls found themselves by the only seats available. One of them stepped over Stryker's legs, dragged her bag across his shins, and plopped down with a huff of exasperation.

Stryker slowly tipped the soiled Stetson up from the bridge of his nose with a long, tanned forefinger.

The girls, busily settling their butts on the bench seat and arranging the luggage, failed to notice him looking at them. When they finally did, the expressions on their faces displayed surprise, fear, or both.

"Sorry, sir," the fairer of the two managed to say. She scrunched up her face and cocked her head to one side when Stryker failed to respond.

"I'm Belle," said the other one. Belle placed the last bag on the floor and nodded toward her friend. "Her name's Lake."

"Could you move your legs, please?" Lake asked, sounding somewhat irritated. A girl in her early twenties, Lake had clear white skin, green eyes, and straight, dark blonde hair, cropped to curl underneath the jawline. Though not real skinny, she had small breasts. She shrugged her shoulders and glanced at Belle when Stryker lowered the Stetson's brim again.

Belle looked a little older, a little darker skin, and firmer in the body. "Hand me your bag. I'll put it over here."

Instead, Lake leaned forward, within two feet of the Stetson, and tipped it up with her forefinger.

Stryker lifted his face and opened his eyes.

"Excuse me, mister badass," she whispered. "Would you mind moving your fucking legs?"

Stryker drew his legs back under the bench and scooted closer to Lake. He reached down and swept the carpetbag from the floor. Getting to his feet, he stepped over to the window and lowered it.

"No!" Lake screamed, realizing he was about to toss her bag out the window. "That's my grandmother's." Lake jumped up and grabbed the bag, wrapping her arms around its Victorian fabric. When Stryker heaved the bag, Lake went with it and fell on Stryker's bench.

Other passengers twisted and turned about, craning their necks to see the commotion. Lake lowered her voice. "It's all Mam'ma has left." She clutched the bag to her chest. Stryker released the handle.

"Leave the bag, and get out of my seat," Stryker said.

"You won't throw it? They're my grandpa's things. He died, and I'm taking them to my grandma in Saint Louis. Belle, reach another bag over here."

Belle picked up one of the bags from her pile and threw it across the aisle. Lake, still holding her grandfather's belongings, got up and stepped around Stryker, exaggerating the space needed to get by him, and plumped down indignantly.

Stryker remained standing long enough to survey the other passengers. Those still looking decided it was a good time to face forward. The men who'd seen Stryker board the train may have noticed how low the Peacemaker hung on his hip, and how quickly it could come out its holster. They opted to not interfere. Satisfied, he'd be left alone, Stryker sat. He leaned on the travel bag now next to him, stretched out his legs again, and lowered the hat brim.

Belle and Lake threw what-the-hell glances at each other and shrugged their shoulders.

Passing outside the windows, the landscape, rolling hills and sparse trees, became dark shadows. The night dragged on. Monotonous wheel clacking caused many of the passengers to drift off. Belle and Lake, their nerves still on edge, remained awake, watching the man across from them. Belle reached for Lake's hand and patted it reassuringly. Then she continued to hold it.

"Is he asleep?" Lake mouthed silent words to Belle.

Belle shook her head side to side. "I don't know," she mimed in return.

They were shocked when Stryker lifted his hat and said, "No."

"We thought you were asleep. Did we wake you?" Belle whispered to him, offering an apology.

"You're afraid to sleep, think I'll throw the bag out," Stryker said.

"No!" Both girls said at the same time. The couple behind them shifted into more comfortable positions but stayed asleep. "No, we don't," Belle whispered. "We didn't, think you'd do that. Did we Lake?" Lake shook her head no.

"Tickets please," the conductor announced as he entered the front of the car. "Have your tickets out as I come through." The portly ticket master outfitted in the conductor's uniform, watch with chain and all, began down the aisle swinging from side to side as he punched the tickets. Occasionally he asked destinations and nonchalantly nodded when told travel plans. He lingered by Lake and Belle briefly.

"Going all the way to Saint Louie?" He asked.

"Yes," Belle said.

The girls got the nod. The conductor punched Stryker's ticket without comment and went out the back door.

"Get some sleep." Stryker raised a hand to drop the brim.

"We really can't right now. Where you going?" Belle asked.

"What's your name?" Lake added before Stryker could reply.

Stryker dropped his arm.

"Stryker. Laws."

Puzzled, Lake asked, "Which one is your name? Are you a lawman?"

"Name's Stryker. Laws is a town."

"We're going to Saint Louis," Lake whispered with a little less anxiety.

"We already told him that!" Belle whispered curtly.

"Oh yeah, I forgot," Lake said sheepishly. "You married?" She asked with a little more enthusiasm.

"Lake!" Belle scolded at the top of a whisper as she saw Stryker's face tighten.

Lake saw it too. "No family either?"

Stryker shook his head once. "Don't like kids."

"Oh? Why not?" Belle showed more interest in the conversation.

"They get in the way of fucking the mother."

Shock, anger, and then humor, flashed on their faces in rapid succession. Both girls tried not to laugh. "Why are you going to Laws?" Belle asked, battling a smile.

Stryker saw no reason to not tell them, and he saw none *to* tell them. "Business."

"You do business with that gun?" Lake's eyes sparkled. Maybe the idea of deadly gunplay excited her.

"You're coming from San Francisco." Stryker glanced out the window.

"Yes," Belle answered, glad Stryker changed the subject. "Lake and I lived there three years."

"My grandfather had a fish restaurant on Powell Street," Lake added. "It was-is, near the wharf. Called the Salty Dog and we helped Gramps in the dining room. You know it?"

"No." Stryker sounded as if he couldn't give a shit. He lifted his hand to the hat, dipped it, and settled against the bag again.

Undeterred, Lake continued. "It's closed now. Gramps never made an effort to pass it on after he died. Guess he planned on living forever." She took a deep breath and blew out. The futility of carrying on the conversation began to register. "We're taking his personal things to . . . Grandma." The final words dribbled out her mouth and died on her lips. She fell back against the backrest and folded arms across her chest, staring at Stryker with resignation.

After a few minutes, Belle placed her arm around Lake and pulled her friend closer, as if to provide comfort. Lake rested her head on Belle's shoulder.

Hours passed and sometime in the dead of night the conductor came through the coach announcing they were pulling into Stockton. Only one elderly couple and two middle-aged women remained in the car. The four sat up near the front. An old man boarded, and positioned himself directly behind the two matronly females.

Stryker raised the Stetson once during the stop, to see who got off and on. Afterward, he continued his light dozing.

Lake, who slept snuggled next to Belle, woke and looked out the window as passengers left the train. When Lake lifted her head, Belle woke up too. They both watched without speaking, tired, still half asleep. After the train pulled away from Stockton, Belle turned away from the window to gaze upon Lake's face faintly lit in the moonlight. Lake extended the tender moment with a smile. They kissed. Not a brief peck, it was a long passionate kiss carried out between two lovers.

When the kiss finally ended, they remained in a tight embrace and caressed each other's faces lovingly. Presently though, they got a feeling they were being watched. And they were . . . by Stryker.

"Enjoying yourself?" Lake asked. The girls broke apart and faced the mixed-breed, trying not to show their embarrassment.

"Could be."

"Uh, well, we like men too." Belle said, somewhat apologetically.

"We share." Lake added.

"We try not to be concerned about a man coming between us," Belle said, as a matter of fact.

The corner of Stryker's lip twitched.

"We live life, enjoy life." Belle stated. "We live to live, not like you." She ventured a thin probe. "You live to die, Stryker. I can see it in your face."

Stryker suddenly sobered. A memory flashed across his mind. Some people in the past had told him, "You haven't lived until you do this, or try that," as if they could persuade him to act a certain way. And then he thought, *you haven't died until you realize you'll never again see your wife laugh again*. The girl was right, he was living to die.

Stryker lowered the Stetson and wrestled with his own thoughts.

Belle and Lake, their passion having waned for the night, wiggled their bodies into comfortable positions, and slipped into an easy slumber.

During the night the Southern Pacific climbed up and over the Sierras before lumbering down the eastern slopes toward Truckee. For some reason not addressed between Belle and Lake, they remained seated on the bench across from Stryker. Perhaps they wanted to keep a watchful eye on the luggage bag under his arm. Nevertheless, conversation was virtually non-existent even after the two women came awake to see Stryker staring out at the window. It now seemed as if a cloudy barrier floated between them and the man kept the words locked behind his tight lips. When the train rolled to a complete stop in Reno, Stryker rose and stepped off the coach, without a salutation. He headed back along the cars, searching for the cattle car holding the roan. Finding it, and bringing the animal up for transfer to the Virginia-Truckee line to Carson City, Stryker was met by the conductor. He handed Stryker a folded piece of paper.

"Them two women gave me this to give to you and took off lickety-split." The rail man displayed no hint of humor.

The note read, "We're spending two days in Reno, and maybe a few more up around Lake Tahoe. We'll be at the Four Poster B&B for the first two nights. Welcome to join us, B and L."

"You'll be staying here, sir?" The conductor asked, as he signaled the engineer up the line.

"No," Stryker answered.

Later that morning, Stryker stepped aboard the Virginia-Truckee with great effort.

CHAPTER FOUR

Miners filled most of the seats in the coach. Although Virginia City mines had seen their best days, men still traveled from as far away as Europe to dig in the barren hills of Reno and Carson City. These days however, the riders weren't the excited, exuberant men who used to crowd into the rail cars in the 1870s. A more somber group sat in the car. Not as many now; everyone had a place to sit. Desperation hung like smoke in the saloons they frequented. Men sat quietly alone, and in the blankness of their faces, they looked hopeless, taking one last attempt out of poverty. Stryker gazed at the miners, wondering how many might be successful, or how many would leave poorer, or how many would die in a black dank hole. He studied the hapless men, already bent from years of worry. He'd seen men, women, like these before, everywhere, people who trudged through life with no apparent goal other than to stay alive. He didn't know whether to feel sorry for them, or to scorn them. A good many brought their misery on themselves, but Stryker didn't waste time judging others. That, he left to a final judgement, if there was one. As for himself, he survived as well; however, he was good with a gun.

Stryker left the train when it stopped at Mound House, leaving the miners to search for fame and glory in Virginia City, and he transferred to the Carson-Colorado, or C.C., line. The C.C. line headed south to Carson City and from there, on south to Laws. The tracks only ran to Keller, some fifty odd miles south of Laws, never reaching the Colorado River or California. The mines they were to service played out before the tracks got to them. However, Stryker only bought a ticket to Hammill, one stop shy of Laws, thinking he should ride the roan into Laws. He figured a man just passing through town would be walking or on a horse. Hearst wanted no connection to Stryker, and a drifter who wandered into town, stayed on a few days probably wouldn't seem a likely emissary for a senator. Stryker also needed time to assess the water problem in Owens valley. He'd have to make contact with Gunner Gaines too. How, when, and under what circumstances, he hadn't decided yet.

Stryker hauled the roan off the train as well. Why the train stopped in Hammill, a small community with only a few scattered buildings, was lost on the mixed-breed. Regardless, it suited his purposes, because he got off and unloaded his horse without drawing attention. The train chugged on without a face in a window too. Stryker's coach car had but one passenger–him, and he doubted the other cars had many riders either. Good, they might have been curious as to why he disembarked in Hammill only to ride into Laws later. He'd planned on spending a few days in Hammill for just that reason, but he hadn't known it wasn't even a town. He swung into the saddle and started south on the trail running along the tracks.

Owens valley, a wide expanse of lush meadows between the Sierra Nevada's to the west and the White and Inyo mountains to the east. The train had passed through the Inyo's, and Stryker now rode on level ground. The trail veered about a quarter mile away from the tracks to pass near streams running like veins through the valley. Although late in summer, snow still crowned the Sierra's, adding a brilliant white to the rich green meadows, forested hills, and the azure sky. Nothing, Stryker thought, as he surveyed the natural beauty, could match this in San Francisco.

He needed a plan to contact Gaines. The sun would soon dip below the Inyo's, and Stryker stopped to make camp near a creek he'd been trailing for the last half mile. Water, a cluster of cottonwoods for shade, and dead branches lying about for firewood looked suitable. What kind of cover would he use in Laws? He knew nothing of farming, or ranching, or any useful job he could do in town, and he couldn't pretend to be a drifter too long. He had army training, military tactics, artillery fire, and close combat—all skills for killing men. Not exactly handy in civilized society. He stashed the Peacemaker in the saddlebag before entering town. At least he wouldn't *appear* to come in looking for trouble.

He unsaddled the roan, put on a halter, and staked the horse near the creek. That's when he heard the singing. Female voices sang low and sorrowful. He recognized the hymn, "Amazing Grace." Winding his way through the cottonwoods, he emerged from the trees and came to a small grassy opening two hundred feet in diameter. A feint wagon trail ran into it on the right, and Stryker guessed the trail led back to the main trail he'd been riding. A Conestoga sat parked in the middle, its mules roped off a few feet from the creek. Three female Negroes stood on the far side of the wagon and Stryker angled right to get a better view.

A Negro man lay at their feet. Two of the women facing Stryker saw him, but they returned their attention to the man on the ground and kept singing. When the hymn ended, one of the women who'd seen Stryker nudged the woman with her back to him. Startled, she spun around quickly. She saw Stryker some thirty feet away, watching them.

"Mister, whatcha want?"

"He sick?" Stryker came closer.

The stricken man moaned. The totally bald Negro with a white beard lay on his back. He had a grotesquely swollen hand resting on his chest. His legs were splayed out toward the creek. Drenched clothing clung, still dripping, to his skin.

"Elvin got bit by a snake, on the hand there," the tallest woman said. She nodded at the swollen hand.

"Jumped backwards and landed on that rock," Another female added. She pointed at a barrel-sized rock, in the water crowned with a jagged ridge. In a sign of mournful resignation, she dropped her arm and let it fall heavily to her side. "Can't feel nothing in his legs."

"Mister." The Negro struggled mightily to lift his eyes toward Stryker.

Stryker looked down at him.

"Dyin' hea'." When no one disputed that, he blinked once, letting his eyes linger closed for a bit, and then he continued, weaker than before. "You . . . if any good . . . in you . . . take 'em on to . . ." The words died on a feint breath, his last one.

"Bishop Creek." The tall one said, finishing for the stricken man. "Gonna sang at the church."

Stryker knelt, laid three fingers on the old man's neck, and stood without speaking.

"Elvin's dead?" Two of them asked together. The short one brought her hand to her mouth, her face contorted in fright.

Stryker scanned their faces. He figured them fearful of being left alone, with no Elvin. Even though the old man couldn't provide much in the way of physical protection, his counsel must have made up for it. Stryker swung his eyes toward the side of the wagon. "Brother Elvin and the Righteous Sisters" was scrolled in a big arc with crosses of different sizes accenting the bright gold letters.

"Sung his last song," Stryker allowed.

"Elvin didn't sang." The three of them said, more or less together.

"Preacher," Stryker said.

"No, he ain't no preacher neither." The tall one volunteered.

Stryker cocked an eyebrow.

"He just read from the good book in 'tween us sanging," she explained.

"What we gonna do now Eula?" The sister next to her asked, looking at Elvin's body.

"Don't you worry none, Hany," Eula said. "We gonna be all right." But those last words of assurance dribbled from her mouth, landing on the dirt. "You help us bury Elvin, mister?"

Stryker found a poor excuse for a shovel in the wagon and dug a hole three foot deep. The women put rocks on the mound to keep animals from digging up the grave. A cross fashioned from a couple of tree limbs marked Elvin's last resting place.

"We be thanking you sir," said Eula, wiping her hands on the back of her dress. "I reckon we ain't been introduced, proper 'an all. Burying

Elvin and us a worrying about what we gonna do now caused us to . . . I'm Eula." She stuck out her hand. When Stryker didn't respond, she waved it toward another sister. "This here is Hany." Hany made busy dusting off her hands. "And Jemima." Eula simply dipped her head, dispensing with hand movements altogether. "And what might your name be, Sir?" Eula asked, sharpening the edge a little.

"Elvin."

The Righteous Sisters looked at each other, canting their heads, their lips forming silent Os.

"You sangin'?" Eula exclaimed. Hany and Jemima abruptly turned to Stryker, their Os morphing into broad smiles.

"No. I read."

"You'd read from the Good Book for us? I mean with us?" Eula asked, her voice scaling skyward.

"That old man mark the words," Stryker said.

It took Eula a moment to realize he'd asked about the passages to read.

"Yes! Good Lordy in heaven be praised! Blessed Father, thank you! Mista' Elvin, you sent by God! Elvin's Bible, it's all showed for ya. We all can't read, but poor Elvin, I mean poor departed Elvin could read. Said he taught his-self." Eula's eyes drifted to the grave. Her eyes softened, giving poor departed Elvin a tender smile. "I reckon we oughta move on a ways Mista' Elvin."

The *living* Elvin drove the gospel wagon, with the roan tied behind. Eula assumed her place beside Stryker while Jemima and Hany crowded close behind them, singing gospel songs. Sometimes Eula would join in. The new Elvin didn't sing.

"Poor ol' Elvin, I mean the *old* Elvin!" Hany lamented, and then clarifying which Elvin was poor. "He worked the plantation for since he was twelve, he said. Forty year, he said. I don't think he ever knew, cause he tolt me he was only forty-three, last January. I guess he forget he already said how long he be in Georgia. He told me that though, when he wuz tryin' to start somethin'."

"Don't talk ill of the dead, Hany," Eula said, glancing sideways toward Stryker. All three women were rail thin and could be justly called somewhat attractive. Hany and Jemima looked as if they could be sisters in their early twenties. Eula had maybe four or five years on them. They may have had an ancestor warm a master's bed longer than necessary. Noses ran straight and narrow.

"I ain't talking ill, Eula. I liked Mista Elvin. I ain't liked 'im that-a-way though. But, I'm gonna miss them stories he used ta tell."

"Me too," Jemima added.

Stryker drove the Conestoga, keeping his thoughts to himself. Taking the role of Elvin might be risky, but he figured his looks would probably draw attention anyway. Hell, put his *Elvin* out there and let 'em deal with it. He got an opportunity to disguise himself, and he took it.

"Tell me how the singing goes." Stryker snapped reins on the mules.

"It's not regular Sunday preachin' you know," Eula started. We does our sangin' at revivals 'an such. They's havin' one in Bishop Creek for ten days or so. I ain't sure. So, we's sangs at 'em. Sangs one or two before preachin', then other'n at tha end of tha words. Sometimes tho, we just do our sangin' an' they don't have no preachin'."

"And Elvin reads then."

"He reads somethun' an' then we sang. He don't do no sangin' causin' he's awful at it. He just kinda moves a little with tha music whiles we sang. We do sangin' at tha end too. That's when they doing tha savin', ya know, savin' peoples from damnation an' such."

"Forgive 'em for they know not what they do," Stryker murmured.

"Whaz that Elvin?" Hany asked. Eula heard the words well enough too, but kept her ruminations inside her head.

Stryker only drove the wagon about a mile and guided it once again closer to the creek. A full moon now cast shadows. He quickly built a cooking fire and then tended to the animals while Eula and Hany boiled potatoes and fried strips of salted pork over the fire. Jemima filled the coffee pot with water from the stream and placed it on two flat rocks she'd spaced apart in the hot coals. The four ate without much conversation.

Later, after food and coffee, Eula, who sat on the only camp stool said, "Elvin, we been talking and we all think we oughta do some prac-ticin' a'fore we gets ourselves up in front of peoples." Hany and Jemima joined Eula, as the three stared blankly at Stryker, waiting for a response.

Stryker reached for the coffee pot and poured the last dregs in his cup. *Shit*. He didn't know how the charade would go, but he'd have to figure some way to carry it off. He was starting to regret this Elvin thing.

"All ya have to do is read words from Elvin's Bible. I mean our Elvin, our old Elvin. We like our new Elvin now. Don't we?" Eula nodded to Hany and Jemima, vigorously bobbing their heads.

"I'll get Elvin's Bible. I mean, uh-," Jemima stammered.

"Just bring it, Jemima," Eula said, exasperated.

Jemima jumped up and ran to the wagon. She returned and presented the Bible to Stryker on upturned palms. He accepted it with the same manner of reference. The book was old, really old. The page edges had grown brown over the years from Elvin's thumbing. Pages within were worn flimsy and delicate. Purple ribbons marked passages to be read. Eula moved beside him with a lantern. She lowered it next to the Bible, and Stryker saw the underlined verses. He hadn't read much of the Bible. What exposure he did have with it was with Leigh. He'd never come close to embracing the meanings within, and he'd strayed, or rather, was driven further away after she died. However, he didn't question another's beliefs. Who was he, he figured, to impose unknowable notions on someone else? He left people and their beliefs alone and demanded the same from them. Stryker chose not to interfere with the righteousness of the Righteous Sisters.

"One more thing, Elvin," Eula said nonchalantly, perhaps hoping the request which followed, would land softly on the mixed-breed. "We all wear our white angel's robes like I done told you." She paused.

Stryker set the Bible aside. He glanced at Hany and Jemima. He glared at Eula.

"Well, you can't jus' wear them clothes." Eula arched her eyebrows at her two sisters, soliciting help.

"Elvin wore a God-damn angel suit." Stryker growled.

"No, but he did strut abouts in a white outfit. An' good gracious, but you'd look mighty fine in it–better no doubt." She cocked her head at Hany and Jemima, "Wouldn't he?"

"Yes, he shore would!" The girls exclaimed.

"You be a little taller an' you ain't got the belly, so we'd hav' ta do a little mendin', but that won't be no trouble. Go fetch it Jemima."

Jemima leapt to her feet and ran to the back of the wagon. She returned with a white, one-piece suit draped across her outstretched arms.

"You should try it on Elvin," Eula said, nodding her head up and down, reinforcing the suggestion.

Stryker remained seated on his saddle, studying the costume. That's what it seemed to him, a costume, a ridiculous *fucking* costume.

"Elvin had us make the bottoms bigger so he could fit it over his boots, and the collar high and stiff cause he had marks on his neck from the whippings. It was my idea to put little stars on it. It ain't got no wings like ours do, so I sewed some different colored stars on like he was going to heaven too. We washed it up for him 'fore we left Virginia City. That's where we did our last sanging. You'll looks good in it and we all be wearing white together," Jemima said, with much encouragement.

"Jesus H. Christ," Stryker allowed, slowly stretching out the Son of God's name. Usually, he withheld such outbursts, but even he had his limits.

"You like it?" Jemima beamed, holding up the suit.

No gunman, or even half a man, would be caught dead in the thing. What self- respecting man would wear that silly outfit? "I like it."

"We knew you would," Hany exclaimed.

Stryker tore his eyes from the outlandish suit. "Alright, here's the deal ladies. If asked, you tell folks I joined you earlier this year. That's all you know. That's all you say. Don't ask why." He said, giving a menacing look to each sister.

The Righteous Sisters glanced at one another, shrugging their shoulders. "Yessar, Elvin," Hany and Jemima said in unison, nodding their heads their heads in agreement.

"Fine by us, Elvin," Eula added. "Will you try it on now?"

Stryker did, and suffered through the fitting adjustments without too much grumbling, figuring that would only slow the measuring.

The following morning, they broke camp and continued south through Chalfant Valley toward Laws. Mid-day they veered away from the trail and stopped near the creek to rest and water the animals. Stryker urged the women to be quick about their tasks and personal attentions because he wanted to make town before nightfall. However, they drove the Conestoga into Laws after sundown. Even in the pale light, Stryker noticed the small community of weathered buildings had seen its best days. There was the train depot, which appeared to be the largest structure, unless one judged a couple of two-story buildings at the edge as bigger overall. Several more buildings lined both sides of the main street, a dirt road that ran perpendicular from the railroad tracks for several hundred yards. Raucous laughter gushed onto the street from a squat, one story hut of a building halfway down on the east side. Stryker figured the noise and lantern light coming through the open door was from a saloon. It looked to be the only one open. A one saloon town couldn't be much of a town he thought. He couldn't see the purpose for the rest of the buildings, not enough light. It didn't seem as if any of them would offer lodging for the night so he wheeled the wagon around and drove farther down the trail, and then off toward the creek to set up camp.

Later, Stryker, Hany, and Jemima sat by the cooking fire, finishing the last of supper. Eula stood pensively across the fire from Stryker, watching him with her arms folded across her chest. She held a cup of coffee in her hand, but she was so engrossed in her thoughts, she neglected to drink from it.

"We'll go on to Bishop Creek tomorrow. I'll ride back into Laws first, pick up a couple of things, ask around." Stryker studied his coffee cup as he spoke. "It's only three or four miles from here. I won't be more than an hour or two."

"Elvin?" Eula asked. She paused for Stryker to switch his attention from the cup to her. He didn't. She continued anyway. "You ain't gonna leave us are ya?"

Stryker looked up. It hadn't occurred to him they might think he'd take off the first chance he got. For a moment he pondered doing just that. Then, he said, "No."

The Righteous Sisters cleaned the pots and pans and went off together into the bushes for personal needs. Stryker threw his bedroll down by the fire. He brought his saddle over as well and sat on it to wait for the women. He heard them talking before they reappeared in the firelight.

"Elvin, we done us some talkin' whiles we, you know, takin' care of ourselves," Eula began. "An' we wuz wondering. We all wuz, ain't that right?" Eula nodded her head at her two sisters who responded back with tentative shakes of their heads. "Now Elvin, don't you take no offense at what I gonna say, but you don't come off lookin' too friendly." Not waiting for Stryker to respond, Eula rushed on. "Church folk act friendly. Like, they act friendly to one other, smiling and such. An' Elvin, you ain't cracked even a hint o' one." She noticed Stryker's countenance growing darker. "I guess I'm saying sometimes you can look kinda mean, Elvin."

Hana and Jemima looked worried.

"You lookin' that way now Elvin." Eula pressed her luck.

Stryker rose, threw the rest of his coffee on the fire, and dropped the empty cup next to his saddle. He made quick strides over to where the roan stood hobbled. "You wear that silly outfit and you can smile at 'em." Stryker groused to the horse. He removed the leather straps from the roan's ankles and led it to the creek. "Damn, what I do for a friend," Stryker grumbled, as the horse drank. *Hearst is a friend?* He asked himself. Stryker had never had friends. It seemed odd to think of Hearst that way. Well, the man had saved his life from loggers bent on killing him. So, he owed Hearst. That doesn't make a friend, whatever the hell that is. Still, he respected Hearst, a self-made man, a tough, rugged individualist. And the Senator had paid Stryker well, extremely well, for securing the *Examiner* for his son, William. He'd also rescued Morgan. That counted for something too. So, was Hearst a friend? No, Stryker had no friends. He never would have. He just used his guns and blades to repay a debt, and he always paid his debts.

"I'll bed down over there," Stryker said, as he walked back to the women, thumbing his hand toward the roan.

The Righteous Sisters glanced at one another and shrugged their shoulders.

The sun rose early over the White Mountains the next morning, but Stryker had already built a cooking fire, made coffee, and saddled the roan by the time its rays crawled from peak to base of the Sierra Mountains to the west. He drank a cup of hot coffee and waited until Eula emerged from the wagon before he climbed on the roan for the short ride back to Laws. He tipped the brim of the Stetson and goaded the roan.

Eula stood by the fire, warming her hands, and watched the mixed-breed ride off. Her eyes followed him until he disappeared around a bend on the trail. She sat on old Elvin's stool, placed by the fire the prior night, and leaned over for the coffee pot. She steadied the cup Stryker left on the flat rock and filled the cup half full. Holding it between her hands, several long minutes passed before she drank.

"He coming back?" Eula failed to hear Jemima coming up behind her.

"Don't know Jemima." Eula didn't need to turn around to know it was Jemima asking. "He ain't actin' none too happy 'bout wearin' 'em clothes."

"What we gonna do if he don't?"

"He ain't comin' back," Hany said, climbing out of the wagon. "He ain't sangin' with us niggers."

"Jemima, fry up some ham," Eula said.

Stryker retraced the trail he and the women had taken, crossing two creeks as he rode back to Laws. He hadn't appreciated the area's beauty the night before. The sun had set when they came down earlier, but he could see the landscape in the bright morning sunlight. The wide valley had multiple streams coursing through it like watery veins supplying nourishment to cottonwood and willow trees amidst the tall, green waves of grass. Off to the west, snowmelt from the white-capped Sierras, kept streams flowing year-round. Abundant wildlife such as white-tailed deer and prong-horn antelope often grazed in the lush vegetation. Farther down the valley streams merged to form the Owens River which itself emptied into Owens Lake, a two-hundred square mile natural reservoir of water brimming with trout. Birds of all kinds and by the hundreds of thousands made regular pilgrimages to the lake. Many people called the bountiful, idyllic scenery of the nation's deepest valley, the *American*

Switzerland. Eventually, two men from Los Angeles would turn the valley into a wasteland.

When he'd ridden out of sight from the Sisters, he halted the roan and dug the gun belt and Peacemaker from the saddlebag. He strapped the gun belt around his waist. Elvin would not last long, he decided.

Stryker rode into Laws from the south and onto Silver Canyon Road, the town's main street. He hadn't seen its sign last night. Mature cottonwoods dotted along the street. A decade earlier nine hundred people had called Laws home. That was when they shipped lumber, supplies, and food to the mines. Now, the mines were played out, and only around four hundred stubborn citizens remained, scratching out a living cattle ranching and farming. But Laws lay on the eastern side of the valley where soil wasn't as fertile. Many folks gave up and moved four miles to Bishop Creek. However, the train still rolled through town, just not as often as before. The town seemed even more tired in daylight. More than a third of the buildings were boarded up. Stores, homes, and even saloons had boards across windows and doors. Some looked vacant and had no boards. It looked as if whoever owned or lived in them, just walked out one day and never came back. A few businesses like Laws General Store still clung to life. Stryker pulled the roan up in front of the store.

What appeared to be two worn out prospectors, sat on wooden chairs each side of the door, with their backs leaning against the wall. Shabby clothes, shaggy hair, sunbaked skin, and foot long beards suggested they had yet to hit pay dirt. Neither spoke. They stared at Stryker as he swung off his horse and walked between them into the store. Then they leaned over and looked through the door.

Stryker saw five more inside, including the store clerk. Off to his left, three men and a boy next to a potbellied stove hovered around a small round table with a checkerboard. The boy, who looked to be no more than twelve years old, sat opposite a man perhaps in his fifties intensely studying the board. The two players sat on nail kegs, hunched over the faded checkerboard. Two old codgers stood and watched the game wearing amused smirks. The youngster played black, his adult opponent, white. Black appeared to outnumber white.

"Need shells for a .44 Colt," Stryker said to be-speckled proprietor behind the counter. Lots of empty shelves hinted that the requested ammunition may not be available. The store clerk remained bent over the counter, writing on a ledger of some sort, and making no indication he heard the request. When he finally looked up to see Stryker, he dropped the pencil, and spun around to open a cabinet door.

".44-40's here," the clerk said, shoving a box of cartridges onto the counter. "They'll fire in a Winchester '73, too. You want the whole box?"

"How much?"

"Two dollars." The clerk noticed Stryker didn't appear pleased. "We're . . ., we ain't that close to the Hartford factory, sir. Dollar-fifty?"

Stryker was digging out the money when he heard thumps on the checkerboard followed by a gravelly voice. "Shit!" He turned to see the kid jumping the fourth white checker in a row. The loser's curse was followed by boisterous laughter from the other two men.

"That Gaines boy ain't lost yet," the clerk said, nodding his head in the boy's direction.

Stryker had no coins in his pocket, so he slapped two dollars on the counter and picked up the box of .44's. He turned away but stopped. "Who's that kid's father?"

The grateful clerk was eager to reply. "Gunner, Gunner Gaines." Then he added, "An' I'm called Jonas, just in case you be in town for a while."

"One of them," Stryker asked, without sounding like it.

"No sir. His pap's away. The boy's here in Laws with his aunt til Gunner gets back. Gunner and his family live down in Bishop Creek. You need anything else? I ain't got change on me right now. You got a fifty-cent credit."

"The mother."

"She's here too, with her cousin." A frown suddenly appeared on Jonas's forehead. "Mister, why you askin'? You know Gunner?" He began to think he'd said too much.

"No." Stryker eyed the boy as he leaped off the nail keg and ran to the counter.

"All right, Shane. Here you go." Jonas reached into the glass jar on the countertop and pulled out a stick of hard Sassafras candy. "I give him a piece of candy when he wins." Grinning big, he chortled, "I'm gonna run outta candy!"

Stryker trailed Shane out the store and took note of which way he ran. Shoving the box of shells in his saddlebag, Stryker peered over the roan's rump and saw him at the western edge of town on Silver Canyon Road. The youngster ran into a small yard surrounded by a short, white picket fence, and up the steps to a green two-story house. The home, standing alone and sheltered by full-grown cottonwoods, was the only two-story building at that end of town.

As Stryker buckled the saddlebag flap, he spotted a barber's pole across the street. He ran a hand on his stubble. He came out of the barbershop twenty minutes later with a fresh haircut and a shave. The drooping mustache survived the encounter and his hair still touched the shoulders. The roan got a whiff of the lilac water and snorted his displeasure.

Stryker mounted up and started out of town. Coming to the cutoff south to Bishop Creek, he saw Shane and a woman by the greenhouse, trimming what looked like a rosebush in the front yard. A gentle pull on the reins and pressure from the left knee kept the big horse heading down Silver Canyon road.

Shane saw Stryker first. "Mamma, it's him." he said ominously. Getting to his feet, Shane whispered, "That man in the store, it's him."

The woman rose and wrapped a reassuring arm around her son's shoulders.

Stryker allowed the roan to pull up a few steps from the two. He leaned forward and rested his forearms on the saddle horn.

The woman sensed he waited for her to start. "My son saw you in the hardware store."

"Gunner about." Stryker said.

"Close by."

"Friend of his asked me to pay him a visit."

"A friend?" She asked, edged with suspicion.

"Man named Hearst. Gunner wrote him."

Relief spread over her face. "My name's Cleo. I'm his wife. This is

Shane." She tugged on Shane's shoulder. "And Gunner didn't write that letter. I did."

Stryker showed no surprise. He remained casually leaning on the saddle horn. Cleo, although not a glowing beauty, had enough about her to warrant a man's attention. Pretty face, however the ample breasts came with an extra twenty pounds on her. She looked to be in her early thirties, but he allowed the woman held up fairly well.

"Want some coffee?" Cleo asked with a smile. When she received no immediate reaction from Stryker, she continued, "Come around in back to the kitchen." She spun the boy around with her. "C'mon, Shane."

Stryker swung off the roan and led it behind him as he followed the mother and son to the rear of the house. Shane took the reins from Stryker and brought the animal to a water trough and rail under a large cottonwood tree standing forty feet back of the house. The horse wasted no time dipping its muzzle in the water trough. "Don't let him drink too much," Stryker said, and he turned toward the house.

Cleo waited by the back steps and studied the tall man as he crossed the yard, the manner in which he carried himself, the smooth and confident way he moved, and-how he wore the Colt .44.

"Mister, whatever your name is, this is my cousin Libra's home. She requests no guns in the house. You can hang it here on the rail." Cleo patted the railing on the back porch.

Stryker hesitated and then unbuckled the gun belt. He didn't offer his name.

Cleo opened the door to the kitchen. She held it open, inviting Stryker to precede her inside. Just as Stryker reached the door, Cleo screamed.

CHAPTER FIVE

Out of the corner of his eye, Stryker caught a glint of the slashing blade. He threw crossed wrists up to block the attack. The Negro with the kitchen knife, was almost as tall as Stryker, and more powerfully built. His well-defined physique was easy to see. He was naked. One muscle below his waist stood out in particular. He had an erection.

Cleo stood in the doorway and screamed. Shane ran up the steps. She shoved him back and kept shrieking.

Stryker had no time to reason out why a naked man with a hard-on would be in the kitchen, attacking him. Using two hands he grasped the thick wrist, pulled it down, and attempted to push it backward in order to rotate under it. He'd used the maneuver before to cause a knife wielder to stab himself. Not this time. He suddenly realized the brute strength of the man. When he tried to push the arm rearward, he couldn't, and the Negro easily raised his arm up with him holding on, to stab again. The naked assailant used his free hand and gripped Stryker's throat.

The two men began a clumsy and violent waltz around the kitchen. Their bodies crashed against the table chairs, breaking them into pieces. The Negro lifted Stryker, threw him against the stove. He felt his ribs crunch when he hit. Still desperately holding off the knife blade with two hands, Stryker was picked up again and driven back against the sink. A bolt of pain shot down his legs. Once more the black man raised him up, heaving him on top the kitchen table. Miraculously, the table held. Added body weight pushed the blade toward Stryker's chest.

Cleo's cousin, Libra, banged open the hallway door and shouted, "Orlo! Put some clothes on!" Upon recognizing the deadly struggle, she weakly added. "For God's sake."

Stryker rolled left, releasing his right-hand grip on the Orlo's massive wrist. The blade plunged into his shoulder. The iron grip on his throat tightened. He faded. He had to be quick. He jammed his hand in his back pocket.

The Negro pushed down harder, twisting the blade. At first, the black man didn't feel the razor in his neck. Then as it sliced deep and across his throat, he sensed something wrong. The razor nicked the carotid artery and sliced through the windpipe. His breathing turned ragged and Orlo's life flowed out of his throat. Then a .44 slug blew out a chunk of his skull.

The roar of the gunshot lifted Cleo's screaming to a high-pitched screech. She cut it off completely as she leapt from the blast. The gunfire shocked the woman to be sure, but the shooter shocked her even more.

"Shane!" Cleo yelled. "What the . . .!"

Shane, holding the Peacemaker in both hands, lowered its barrel.

Cleo and her sister cautiously approached the kitchen table where the two men had struggled. The dead Negro lay on top. Stryker barely clung to consciousness; his head ached from lack of oxygen more than his shoulder with the knife still in it. With great effort, Stryker rolled the dead man off him. He fell back on the table. He heard the women talking. Then their voices drifted away.

"He's got blood all over him. Who is he?" Libra stared at the man with a knife in him.

"You know, he never said," Cleo replied. "What about him?" She walked around the table to look at the dead attacker. "He was in the kitchen when we came in, naked, totally, and with a big hard you know what down there." Cleo pointed at Orlo's groin.

"Orlo, Orlo James. I think he actually came here to rape me, God what a scary thought." Libra folded her arms, nervously rubbing above the elbows. "He's been makin' leering eyes at me. He worked laying rails when they brought the tracks through. Been hanging around doing odd jobs since."

"Shane!" Cleo faced her son in the doorway. "Get the doctor!"

Shane stuffed Stryker's Peacemaker back in its holster and dashed up Silver Canyon Road toward center of town.

⚔

"Well, I tolt ya. He ain't comin' back," Hany groused, carrying the last of the cooking pans to stow in the Conestoga. "We just gonna sit here and wait for him? Or what?" She threw the pans in the wagon where they clattered to the floorboard.

"What we gonna do Eula?" Jemima asked. She leaned against the wagon, looking forlorn, her arms hanging empty by her sides. "We got nowhere to go . . . and nothing to do when we get there."

"He'll be back. Don't you worry," Eula said, staring at the road to Laws. "I believe there's more to him than how the man looks."

"Mean, that's how he looks, got evil, scary eyes" Hany snorted. "Mean, that's what he is, and that's why he ain't comin' back."

"He'll be back," Eula said quietly to herself, still looking up the road. "He'll be back and we need to wait here for him." She spoke convincingly to the other two girls, perhaps in an effort to reassure herself as well.

⚔

A few miles down the road, five men sat in a room at the Bishop Creek Hotel. Two young men with dreams of fame and glory, sought to fulfill destiny. They planned to rescue a thirsty Los Angeles from growth stagnation, by bringing water from Owens Valley to rapidly growing Southern California. The two were Frederick Werner, Los Angeles Water Commissioner and Cole Books, chief civil engineer for the city. The other three men in the room were Bishop Creek locals, municipal politicians, councilmen who own no cattle and no farmland. The room where they all sat wasn't luxurious, but it had a conference table of sorts. Three men sat along the sides with the other two on the ends. Brightly yellow flowered wallpaper covered the walls, and a bouquet of yellow Marigolds, which normally sat on the long table, had been moved to a serving table. The five men finished eating and remained seated, enjoying their coffee. Werner was at one end, Books at the other, with the councilmen, two and one on the sides. Rays of morning sunlight burst in through the window's white linen curtains and brightening and warming the room.

"Well Cole, you got me up here. They have the water. I can see that. Now tell me how to get it, and how to move it two-hundred miles to Los Angeles. Frederick Werner, a square jawed, clean shaven, handsome man sat stiffly upright in the only stuffed chair at the table. Although only in his mid-thirties, Werner's rigid posture and deep voice solicited respect.

"First, we secure the water rights. Our friends here help with that." Books winked at the three councilmen. "And then we build an aqueduct."

"Two hundred miles? C'mon Cole." Werner's booming voice seemed too big for the room.

"Two hundred and thirty-three miles. And it's all downhill," Books boasted with the confidence of a knowledgeable engineer, which he was. "Get the water in the aqueduct and gravity will do the rest." He swept his down-turned palm in front of his body, gesturing flowing water.

"Just like that." Werner mimicked the engineer with his own hand movement. "And all the way to Los Angeles, huh?"

"Won't even need a single pump."

Werner nodded pensively, a wry smile peeped around one corner of his mouth. "If this works Cole, I'll put your name on something, that is, after I'm elected commissioner. Maybe a street." He frowned, but the wry smile remained on his face. "They won't be naming any streets for you here in Bishop Creek."

The councilman seated by himself, closed his eyes and let them linger a brief moment before reopening them.

"You know Edward." Werner knew everyone called Edward Ralston, Eddie. He used "Edward" to needle and belittle. "There's plenty of water for everybody. The folks down south need it too. And my friend, they'll pay you big money." Werner arched his eyebrows at the councilman. "Maybe your family doesn't want it, though. I'll ask your wife."

Eddie married above his station and his wife, Zelda, a woman accustomed to the good life, constantly reminded him he hadn't lived up to her expectations. Edward Ralston, at the time of their marriage, was a handsome catch. A young man of twenty-eight, he was physically fit and glib of tongue. And Edward had his pick of several girls whose knees weakened when he sauntered into a room. That was eighteen years ago. Gaining three pounds a year doesn't seem like much, however after eighteen years of it, angular lines on his face got swallowed in puffy flesh, reddened by heavy alcohol use. His belt buckle had marched out to the last hole as well. And he had yet to distinguish himself in any line of work. Zelda's father, a highly successful rancher, doted on his only daughter, spoiled her actually. Zelda was fond of saying, "The best is good enough for me." She and her father thought that funny. Eddie did too at first, then first faded. This water project could kill two birds with one well-placed stone. He'd get money and her contemptuous father would most likely be ruined. Still, Eddie felt uneasy about the whole thing. With some effort, he collected himself. "I think there is plenty of water for north and south."

The other two councilmen nodded in agreement. Plain old-fashioned greed motivated brothers Peter and Sandy. Their parents taught them to cheat others out of money at an early age. Just doing business, they would say. Unlike Ralston, the two brothers hadn't grown into pudginess over the years. They were always fat.

"Don't say anything right off," Werner instructed. "Cole here has been brought up to Owens Valley at the request of the town council. He'll tell 'em a new irrigation system is needed; one which connects all sources of free-flowing water, streams and wells, so that water can be redirected, redistributed, efficiently to the ranchers and farmers. Of course, we'll have to obtain water rights to do it. By the time the canal is dug out up to here, we'll own the water and there's nothing they can do about it. A thirsty Los Angeles will have the water it sorely needs to grow. We're all depending on you three boys," Werner pointed, as if counting with his forefinger, at Peter, Sandy, and Eddie, "To pull this off. If you do, you three are gonna make a lot of money. And, I mean a lot of it, As long as the water flows, the money flows." Werner smiled grimly.

Broad grins sprouted on two councilmen faces; another appeared on the third councilmen somewhat reluctantly, but surface it did, and grew just as broadly.

Stryker awoke with the doctor putting the last wrapping bandage around his shoulder.

"I poured whiskey on ya, front and back," Doc Wiggins mumbled when he noticed Stryker's eyes blinking open. You might have one of the women douse the wound twice a day for the next two days. An' you might wanna take a snort before. It'll sting a little."

Stryker, still on the table and naked above his waist, rolled onto his good side and pushed himself up to sit. Glancing down beside the table to the floor, he noticed the Negro was gone. A shadow of blood remained on the floor. It would require several more scrubbings to wash out the rest. The table got cleaned too. Maybe not as much blood had to be washed off its surface since Stryker vaguely recalled pushing the black man off him before he passed out.

"Yeah, that boy's gone. Had a couple men from the saloon come over and take him out. They brought that bottle next to you there." Wiggins nodded at a quart of rye whiskey on the table. "And, you can thank Ansel; he owns Ansel's Saloon, with two dollars. You can thank me with three more."

He worked Stryker's left arm into a sling while he talked. "Left it open some. Let bleed a little. Stryker tried to say something in return, but his damaged throat only allowed a whisper. He awkwardly dug into his front left pocket with his right hand and laid dollar bills on the table beside him. Separating out three, he handed the money to Wiggins.

The Doctor picked up the needle and thread, and what remained of a roll of gauze, and placed the items in the black satchel. "You know the man?" He asked Stryker, as he closed the bag.

Stryker shook his head no.

"Hmmm," Wiggins grunted. "Well, he's dead, and I reckon it ain't any of my business. But jus' wondering why his penis was cut off and stuffed in his mouth."

Stryker stuffed the dollars back in his pants. He slid off the table and spied the razor on the sink. He stepped over to retrieve it. The blade had been wiped clean of blood and he slipped it in his back pocket.

Wiggins, figuring he'd gotten all he would get from the mixed-breed, left out the back door of the kitchen.

"He deserved it." Libra deadpanned. Thinner than her cousin Cleo, Libra had the makings of an attractive woman. Something about her though, maybe the way she'd let her hair grow long, reaching waist length down her back, or, how she shuffled her feet flitting about the kitchen, speaking with flowing arm gestures, all of which suggested she tried too hard at being earthy. Indian dreamcatchers of various sizes and colors hung in the two windows and native ornaments set about on counters and tables suggested Libra, who wore a plain, long straight dress, was enamored by the spiritual.

Cleo snapped up her head and threw a puzzled look at her cousin. "He been here before?"

"No." Libra did not elaborate.

Stryker wondered if Libra had gone about town teasing a wolf, a big black one. He let the cousins stare at each other and left to retrieve the Peacemaker. Outside, he saw his shirt hanging on a clothesline that ran from the house to a wooden post in the ground. They'd washed the blood out of it, and it still dripped heavily, making little plops in small mud puddles under the shirt tail. Probably not a good idea to soak the cut, he'd wait. He slipped his arm out of the sling to buckle on the gun belt. Seeing the roan resting in the shade of the cottonwood, he decided to pull a clean shirt from the saddlebags. He attempted to put it on but the pain in his shoulder, which had stiffened considerably, made him feel wobbly.

Try as he might, he couldn't get his left arm in. Sitting on the steps didn't help. He wrapped the shirt around his shoulders. Stepping back inside, the cousins saw the Peacemaker on his hip, however, neither said anything. They also noticed a bare-chested man in control of his body, a badly scarred body. Stryker was a lean man, but his well-defined muscles got regular use. And with the quick, easy way he moved, they may have figured he'd be quick with the Peacemaker.

"Gunner!" Stryker said, sounding as if he had given an order to Cleo, demanding the whereabouts of her husband.

Cleo shifted her attention away from Libra and addressed Stryker. "He's up north. In a valley called Yosemite. He left two weeks ago with another man, a Watkins fellow, Carl Watkins."

"Carleton Watkins," Libra corrected, throwing a clean tablecloth on the table. "The Senator's wife sent him to take photographs there, that's what Carleton told me. Must be some valley for Mrs. Hearst to want pictures of it."

"Mrs. Hearst," Stryker hoarsely repeated. He sought clarification.

"Phoebe Hearst, yes. Wife of George Hearst, Senator of California. Don't you know who our . . .?" Libra stopped her sarcastic rebuke in mid-sentence, perhaps thinking Stryker might have a fragile grasp on civility. And his fearsome countenance also suggested she not annoy him. "Would you like some coffee?"

Stryker pulled out a chair and sat as his answer. Cleo sat as well and Stryker turned to her. "Your husband's a photographer."

"No." Cleo said. Stryker continued glaring at her. "He paints," she began slowly. "He's an artist, thinks he's one anyway. He went up there to paint."

Something in the way Cleo described her husband made Stryker think she wasn't all that happy with his artistry. She sounded a little embarrassed with it, and he sensed a little frustration as well.

Libra placed cups in front of Stryker and Cleo. She poured another for herself and joined them at the table. "It's showin' through, some of the blood, I mean. God, I can't believe we're just sittin' here like nothing happened." Libra moved her eyes around the kitchen as if wondering if it would ever be the same. "When you leave, Cleo, I'll be scared to come in here. Damn. You will stay a few more days, won't you? There are two bedrooms upstairs and one downstairs." She looked at Stryker; however, the mixed-breed's gaze remained on Cleo.

"Of course," Cleo assured her cousin, "Even if Gunner shows up." Although she directed her words at Libra, she looked at Stryker. Finally, Cleo switched her attention from Stryker to her cousin. I think mister . . . knows who Senator Hearst is. She suddenly realized two things. One, she shouldn't say more about why Stryker came to town, and two, she still didn't know his name.

"His name's Stryker, ma," Shane announced coming through the back door. "Major Evil Stryker, that's what it says on his saddle," Shane continued breathlessly. He had just jumped the steps after running across the yard from the roan. He stopped abruptly, sidling up next to his mother.

"It's your horse?" Cleo asked.

Stryker nodded.

"And your name, is it . . .?"

"Neville. Some wore off. Stryker'll do."

"Are you in the Army?"

"Long past."

"We washed your shirt. I'll sew the holes when it dries," Cleo said with a smile. She paused, giving Stryker time to respond with a thank-you or at least some kind of acknowledgement. Stryker said nothing, and the smile slinked off her face.

"Why you asking about Gunner, Mister Stryker?" Libra jumped in.

Stryker swung to Libra. "That's 'tween me and him. Mean 'im no harm." Then back to Cleo. "You haven't said when you expect him."

"I don't really know. He should've been home by now. The ranch needs him here, and Shane misses him too." Cleo didn't say she missed her husband.

"Tell me about this town and the one down the road, Bishop Creek." Stryker sipped from the cup and carefully lowered it to the fresh linen.

"Well, Laws here, is—was, a mining town," Cleo started. "The mines have about given out. Weren't for the railroad there wouldn't be much left. A few years ago, they started bringing cattle up the valley, Owens Valley, and I guess some of 'em decided this would be good cattle raising country, and they began building houses and ranches by the creeks, Bishop Creek's creek." That was silly of me." Cleo smiled sheepishly. "Anyway, that's how that town got born. It's bigger than Laws now."

"You have cattle," Stryker said.

"A hundred or so. Our ranch is six miles east of Bishop Creek." Cleo wrapped her arm around Shane and drew him closer. "Our ranch has two hands and me–and Shane, handle things when Gunner's gone," She said, tussling her son's hair.

Stryker shifted to Libra. "You woman, live here alone."

"Yes," Libra replied with hesitation. "My husband ran off with a girl in a traveling circus five years ago. I don't know what he saw in her." She floated her palm up to twirl the air. "I make a living selling beads an' telling fortunes to women, but I get men who sneak in too."

"I didn't know you told fortunes, Libra," Cleo exclaimed, sounding genuinely surprised.

"Why yes, dear. Palms, I read palms. A person's hands, the lines in 'em, tell all about the past and the future." Libra did a double arm wave. She pressed her palms together, and then threw them in the air, curving her arms around and down an imaginary globe. "The present too, I'm pretty good at knowing what kind of work they do, just by their palms."

"Amazing," Cleo said, sounding less than effusive with praise.

"I know Gunner is a great painter," Libra countered defensively.

"He can't draw water out of a well," Cleo huffed.

"He's beautiful! His work I mean." Libra almost swooned.

Stryker began to regret killing Orlo. No doubt the Negro shoving his enormous shaft up Libra's ass would have done her a world of good.

"I'm getting worried about the beautiful man. Maybe I should send one of the ugly ranch hands to fetch him," Cleo said with sweet sarcasm, and then she gave the mixed-breed a sly grin.

Stryker dodged the hint. "I'll be collecting my shirt now." He rose stiffly from the table.

"It can't be dry already, and I can't sew it wet," Cleo told him. When he started to leave anyway, she jumped to her feet. "Here, let me help you with that shirt." She pulled the shirt from his shoulders and gently lifted his arm from the sling. She worked his arm in the shirt sleeve. He worked in the other one. The shirt tail remained untucked. Cleo kept her back to Libra and silently mouthed to Stryker. "I need to talk to you." Following him through the door outside, Cleo added out loud, "I'll get your shirt off the line," and she hurried to the clothesline with light, quick steps. However, as she reached it, Cleo saw three riders coming in the distance. "There's Gunner!" She forgot the shirt and ran to the edge of the yard. There Cleo stopped, holding her hand as a visor over her eyes. "Thank God he's back . . . I guess," she added, looking a little sheepish. Turning briefly back to Stryker, and then forward again, Cleo watched the approaching riders.

Shane, who'd remained in the kitchen, came out of the house, brushing past Stryker to join his mother.

They came in from the north, riding horses. Each rider had a roped pack mule trailing behind.

"There's Gunner and Carlton. I don't know the other'n." Libra had come outside to stand beside Stryker. "You don't much like me do you," she said, staring at the riders.

"No."

"I don't like you either." Libra waited for a response. She got none. "That man you killed, he wasn't the first, was he?" She knew he wouldn't answer. She asked anyway, letting him know she figured him to be a killer.

Stryker slipped his arm from the sling and let it hang by his side. It hurt like hell. He lifted the arm with his good one and slipped it back into the sling. Watching Cleo anxiously waiting for Gunner, he realized, regardless of her criticism, she cared very much for her husband. For a brief moment, he wondered about that woman, Morgan, in San Francisco, if she waited that way. *Fuck it.* "Name another cattle rancher around here, Libra."

"Another rancher? You looking for cattle? What's wrong with Gunner's?"

"Need more'n a hundred head."

"Well, there's the "BC" brand. The Cavin Ranch, down Big Pine way. I imagine he's got 'nough for ya." Libra swiveled her head and eyed Stryker. "You aimin' to buy 'em or . . . you don't look much like a cattle man, Mister Stryker."

"Not a cattle thief, lady." Stryker stepped off the back porch and strode over to his shirt hanging on the line. He felt the bottom of the shirt. It was still wet. Leaving it, he walked to the roan, stood on the other side, and used his good arm to tuck in his shirttail. He watched as Gunner rode up, dismounted, and embraced his wife. The other two dismounted and led their horses to the water trough next to Stryker and the roan.

"Mornin' mister," Watkins greeted. His eyes dipped briefly to the Peacemaker on Stryker's hip. However, the arm in its sling may have made the fearsome man seem a little less aggressive. "Name's Carleton, Carleton Watkins." Carleton offered his hand, which was ignored, and he dropped it. "And this here is Remy." Remy nodded.

"Stryker." He might have said more, then again probably not, regardless, he saw Cleo pointing his way. She dropped her arm and continued talking. Gunner studied Stryker, while his wife spoke. Eventually, the two of them, with Gunner leading his horse and mule, strode over to the water trough.

"Mister, I want to thank you for what you did this morning." Gunner paused, then asked, "How's the shoulder?" Gunner, had Mexican blood in him like Stryker. He stood a half head shorter, medium build, with a crop of unruly black hair, and glared at Stryker with obsidian eyes.

"Fine."

It took a few moments. Stryker and Gunner locked eyes, each man searching for clues in facial features, rifling through memory files, trying to place when and where they'd known or seen each other. Gradually, and almost simultaneously, recognition crept onto their faces. Only Stryker hadn't known a man called Gunner. This man wasn't Gunner either, and he wasn't Shane's father. He was Elfego Baca. Baca, in his mid-twenties now, would be too young at fifteen to have fathered Shane and started a family with Cleo. Stryker had seen Elfego Baca in Frisco,

New Mexico around six years ago. Baca, a nineteen-year-old Sheriff, held off upwards of eighty angry cowboys in an adobe jacal, or hut, for thirty-three hours. The cowboys sought revenge for the young Sheriffs having killed a rowdy one of their own in a gunfight the day before. However, after firing four thousand rounds into the hut during the night, and losing eight men to Elfego's bullets, the cowboys were surprised to find him calmly cooking eggs and tortillas in the jacal the next morning. Elfego Baca was quick with his gun and had a deadly aim.

Baca's posture grew stiff. He also knew Stryker. The mixed-breed had helped even the odds later that morning. The Sheriff had watched through the hut's new holes as Stryker's bullets introduced themselves to a number of cowboys. The gun fire finally ended. The cowboys gave up. In addition to several getting shot, they'd gotten drunk and weary from lack of sleep. When Elfego came out onto the street, he saw Stryker sitting on a chair propped up in front of the saloon sipping a beer. Total communication before, during, and after that day, between the two men were two head nods as the Sheriff walked past the saloon, and on up the street.

"Gunner," Stryker said. None of his business, if Elfego wanted to be Gunner, fine by him. Cleo probably didn't know of Baca's prowess with a gun either, otherwise she wouldn't have solicited Hearst for help. Perhaps the young gun also scratched a particular itch of Cleo's. So what? Good on them. The art thing though, he doubted the fearless Elfego would be as good drawing a picture as he was drawing a gun. Could be he sought to begin a new life here. He wasn't wearing a gun. However, if the water issue turned violent, Baca would be a good man to have around.

Gunner relaxed with a grin, "Stryker."

"Mister Stryker is stingy with words," Libra said, walking up to the group. "You'd think he paid a lot of money for them and doesn't like givin' 'em away." She flexed the corners of her mouth, hinting a smile. She noticed the growing spot of blood near the top of the sling. "It was my largest kitchen knife, went through him." A genuine look of concern replaced the nascent smile.

"And Shane, I hear you're a brave man too!" Gunner chose "man" instead of "boy," paying the boy a big compliment. Shane stretched taller and beamed a wide grin. It seemed obvious the boy had taken a liking to Gunner. Shane's real father must not have been hard to replace, Stryker reasoned.

"Let's all go in the house and look at what we done in Yosemite," Gunner suggested. "Shane, tie 'em up, will ya?" Gunner handed his horse's reins to the boy and signaled for Carleton and Remy to do the same. Shane pulled the horses away from the water and held them in place while the three *artists* untied the pigtail ropes. He walked them to the cottonwood where Stryker's roan stood hitched to a rail in the shade. They brought the mules to the trough and pulled off the artwork while the animals drank. Shane, without being told, gathered the mules, led them to the cottonwood as well, and hitched them on the rail opposite the horses. The women were already in the house by the time the four men, three of them toting large reinforced leather art cases, headed inside.

"Bring your drawings in here," Libra called from the living room. "We can set them out on chairs where the light is better." Cleo and Libra scrapped chairs on the hardwood floor as Stryker and the artists made their way through the kitchen and down the hall. They emerged into a well-lit room which had a small sun room. A canted bay window protruded out and faced east to capture morning sun light. Kitchen chairs, brought in by the women, were placed in a semi-circle and lined along the three windows.

Cleo and Libra stood back and watched with anticipation as Carleton, Remy, and Gunner unfastened their cases, and selected photographs or paintings for display on the chairs.

Stryker settled into a settee on the opposite side of the living room, curious but not enthralled. He was busy deciding when he should, or could, return to the Righteous Sisters. It looked as if a private talk with Cleo would have to wait, and he might learn about the water situation from someone else, maybe the Cavin man. Regardless, here in Laws, things had gotten complicated with missing husbands and Baca pretending to be one of them. Not one of these people knew everything about the others. He needed to get out of here, do some clear thinking.

Get an outsider's perspective. Armed with more facts, he could wade back in later. Maybe the knife in his shoulder was a pointed hint to move on. Stryker adjusted his arm in the sling.

The men, satisfied with their displays, retreated to the living room, allowing Cleo and Libra to move in and admire the artwork. The two advanced tentatively, as though approaching a casket. They began on the left with the photographs, uttering "ooh's" and "aah's" as they advanced around the sunroom. But the most controversial work, that which elicited the greatest disagreement, was Gunner's. The women stood by his painting a full five minutes as Libra gushed over his work. Cleo seemed puzzled.

Remy and Carleton cast baffled glances at one another while Gunner beamed. Embarrassed, he cut in. "How about some food? We're all mighty hungry here, got bellies growling from the long ride."

Cleo and Libra spun away from the art. "Give us a half hour and we'll fix that," Cleo exclaimed with a laugh. "Go tend to your horses or something. C'mon Libra, show me where everything's at." They swept past the three artists and down the hall. All but Stryker followed, leaving him in the living room alone.

Getting to his feet he strolled over to the sunroom. Yes, the photographs by Watkins were stunning. Giant sheer granite cliffs soared thousands of feet from the valley floor. The photographer had taken pictures at the most propitious times of the day, capturing shafts of sunlight to illuminate the towering walls, making them appear even more majestic. Waterfalls seemed to pour from the sky. They pounded the valley floor below, spraying misted plumes up hundreds of feet. The magnificence of Yosemite was on full display. Watkin's work was brilliant.

Remy's painting; a black and white scene titled *Mule Train Crossing the Sierras* was less majestic, yet vividly realistic. On the canvas a man, perhaps Mexican, sat astride his horse tending to seven or more heavily ladened mules taking water from a mountain stream. The stream flowed out of a rocky slope, suggesting the water ran clear and cool. One could tell Remy seemed comfortable drawing horses and mules. He drew form and proportion accurately. They were depicted well in various positions, with two or three of the rascally beasts drawn with impish expressions.

Gunner's painted landscapes on the other hand, were somewhere between laughable and pathetic. Backgrounds and foregrounds appeared indistinguishable. Mountains, trees, and boulders had been drawn in unnatural shapes. Painted dark strokes bled through the light ones. Was he in a race to finish his work? Remy's paintings and Watkin's photographs drew the observer into the scenes. Their portrayals evoked transference, emotional involvement. Gunner's work screamed incompetence, and art had no chance. For Libra to go on so about his pitiful effort caused Stryker to figure the great Elfego was sinking his shaft in both women.

Maybe Baca had had enough gun play and of having to face every would-be gun slinger seeking fame. Maybe he got tired of looking over his shoulder; not every challenger wanted a fair fight, and in fact most did not. It was well known throughout the southwest that bullets just couldn't find Elfego. Somehow, not one of the thousands of rounds launched at him actually hit him. Or it could be, Baca felt bad, or grew weary, of killing the men who confronted him. Either way, Baca's disguise as an artist, although a really bad one, served him well. And, while living this new life, he tended to Cleo's and Libra's needs.

Stryker discarded the bloody arm sling and hooked his thumb in his belt instead. He left the stained sling hanging on the doorknob and walked out the front door. He glanced down Laws's main street, not much activity there he thought, even though it was well into the day. Quickening his stride, he strode around the house to the roan. Shane had already pulled saddles from the horses and was busy wiping them down with a wet rag. Gunner and Remy weren't around. Stryker figured they were in the house stowing away art, re-arranging the kitchen chairs, and cleaning the mess. Watkins, fussing with the tripods, cursed in frustration, glanced over at Stryker, and went back to fussing and cursing.

"Sorry mister," Shane heard Stryker and came out from behind a horse. "I'd done yours too, only I wasn't sure you'd be needin' him. Guess I was right," He quickly added when Stryker pulled the roan off the rail. "You leavin'?"

"Reckon so. Back later."

Using his injured shoulder to mount brought a stab of pain. He hooked the thumb back in his belt and rode off.

Shane watched Stryker until he'd ridden a half mile and disappeared past a clump of cottonwoods.

CHAPTER SIX

Senator Hearst and Morgan followed the uniformed attendant to the front row of the Savoy Theater. Hearst himself wasn't particularly fond of plays or any of the arts; however, his wife, Phoebe, was traveling in Europe with William, and Morgan liked them. The opening night performance, *Swan Lake* by Pyotr Tchaikovsky, was one Morgan wanted to see. She assumed correctly that Stryker wouldn't take her. The Savoy had been closed for over a month after the previous owners died. The Blanktons produced plays featuring socialist themes that were propaganda statements instead of entertainment productions. Two of the actors, Stan and Myrna Angle, had solicited Morgan's aid in returning the theater back to its intended use. Morgan in turn asked the help of Hearst and Stryker. During the subsequent course of events, the Blanktons lost their lives. Actually, Stryker killed them.

Tonight, Stan and Myrna didn't perform. They worked back stage. Stan considered himself more of an actor than a man light on his feet. Myrna agreed Stan wasn't light on his feet, but he was heavy on hers, so neither danced. Two performers garnering top billing were the Russian star Sergei Kokoff and Pamela Mitchell, an American ballerina being presented on stage for the first time. Hearst had not seen American ballet, or any ballet for that matter. Curious though, he read the *Examiner*'s San

Francisco Arts section which described the performance. He figured people getting turned into swans sounded silly. Pheobe liked this stuff, but *she* couldn't get him to accompany her to a ballet. Morgan took her seat. He sat down beside her and then swiveled for a quick glance. She sat transfixed at the curtains, waiting for them to open with eager anticipation. She felt his eyes on her and turned toward Hearst with a smile. Perhaps he might enjoy the ballet after all, he thought. Pheobe was not as pretty as Morgan.

The theater seated two hundred and eighty people on the sloped floor with another hundred and twenty in the balcony and box seats lining the walls. Directly in front of Hearst and Morgan was the orchestra pit. Its musicians were testing their instruments, getting the audience in the mood. A towering maroon curtain draped to the floor. On it hung the large glittering, gold letters, *ST,* illuminated by a spotlight with its newly invented incandescent bulb. All the guests were seated. The theater hummed with murmurings.

Fifteen minutes after the ballet was to begin, the spotlight dimmed, and the curtains rose. Opening scene took place in a park. Sergei, the prince, celebrated his coming of age with his male friends, all dancing in white tights showing off their muscular legs and bulging scrotum pouches. The revelry ended late in the night and Sergei's friends moved on. Left alone, he was soon visited by the beautiful and graceful Pamela as Odette, a girl who had been turned into a swan by an evil magician. Odette could only take human form at night; by day she lived as a swan. Senator Hearst sat awed by the ballerina's splendor. She floated about the stage, the flowing ends of her white costume danced in the air. She seemed to defy gravity when she leaped, hanging suspended high above the ground, and twirling her feet. Never, he thought, had he witnessed such a lithe and wispy nymph as this dazzling ballerina on stage.

The mesmerized Senator and the rest of the audience failed to notice the shadowy shape slinking along the catwalk high above the deck. The man moved quietly, slowly, searching for something, or someone. Because of the lighting, members in the front rows couldn't see the man in the fly loft. Due to the angle, neither could members farther back, or those in boxes, or in the balcony.

Only one person noticed the illusory figure, Stan. He stood off stage, waiting to arrange props between scenes; he glanced up to check on the lighting. Something up there moved. Stan alone worked the stationary lights above the deck. No one else should be on the catwalk. He moved away from the glare of floor level lighting and searched again. Then, he saw him. Stan chose not to yell. Instead, he quickly stepped to the wall ladder leading to the catwalk and climbed.

He almost reached the top when he heard the gunshot. Scurrying up the last rungs, Stan slipped noiselessly onto the catwalk, and brought himself to a low crouch. Busy taking careful aim for another shot, the assailant, with one eye squeezed shut, failed to notice Stan. When Stan crashed into his side, the gun fired again, striking a can light. Pieces of glass fell to the deck, but the ballet still continued uninterrupted. The two men wrestled on the catwalk. Stan somehow managed to keep the gun pointed away from him and another shot went off as they struggled. That bullet landed harmlessly in the ceiling, but the fourth and final bullet creased the shooter's chest on its path through his chin and into his brain. Stan held on to him and eased the body to the catwalk, keeping it from falling. Blood dripped in heavy blobs, expanding in a dark red pond on the wooden deck below. One dancer even slipped in it, but still, the performance went on.

The first bullet though, had found its mark. Councilman Brower, sitting five seats to the left of Morgan, slumped in his seat and people nearby thought him sleeping, as he often did. But the assailant had gotten lucky, for him anyway, not so much for the councilman. The Colt Lightning .38 bullet lay lodged in his heart. As is often the case, death called upon the lonely. While patrons watched and enjoyed the ballet, Brower passed from living to not living without notice. He did it alone. Not until the performance ended, and the crowd rose to give a standing ovation, did the good councilman's wife realize her husband was dead.

"Why would anyone want to shoot him?" Seated at a table in Tone's Pub across from the Savoy, Pamela posed the obvious question to Stan, Myrna, Sergei, and Morgan. Senator Hearst had gone off to play poker, a recreational pastime more to his liking. "Do you think they were really aiming at him?" Pamela asked, directing the follow up at Morgan.

"Yes." Morgan answered, dryly. She drew a long breath and looked around the table. "He's been a target some time now. Whether a lucky shot or a good one, it was aimed at him."

"Why so, Miss Morgan?" Stan diverted a full glass of Tone Ale away from his mouth and placed it back on the tabletop.

"Referendum question thirteen. In case you don't know, it's to outlaw guns in San Francisco. Councilman Brower was a vocal critic against it."

"That's right!" Stan leaned forward and slammed his fist on the table.

"Ironic," Myrna said. "A man wanting guns was shot by another who didn't."

The others turned toward Myrna, who sat staring at the wineglass in her hand.

"Actually, you make a good point Myrna. If guns are outlawed, people like Brower won't have guns, but criminals will," Morgan commented wryly.

"They're not gonna get my cousin's shotgun, I can tell you that! He goes hunting all the time. Not givin' that up." Stan said firmly, reflecting his cousin's stand on guns.

"Hunting has nothing to do with it, I can tell you that," Morgan said. "I lived in a town taken over by a bad bunch. Said they'd make lives better, that guns wouldn't be needed. So, everyone turned them in. We ended up being slaves. If it hadn't been for Stryker . . .," Morgan stopped in mid-sentence.

"Who's Stryker?" Pamela asked.

"Yeah, who's Stryker?" Stan repeated. "Senator Hearst once told us he had a man who could help with the Blanktons. That him?"

Morgan said nothing.

"I thought they . . . the paper said Blankton fell and Mrs. Blankton hanged herself. You mean that's not what happened?" Stan asked, looking puzzled.

"Blanktons and people like them won't ever quit," Morgan said grimly. "We'll be fighting them a hundred years from now. They need power. They thirst for it like you do water. They take it and get drunk on it. And when they do, the rest of us suffer. The meek can't stop 'em." Her face hardened, and she looked at each person at the table, ensuring they understood.

"We just want to act." Stan laid a reassuring hand on his wife's.

"And I just want to dance!" Pamela exclaimed.

"We all just want to live our lives." Morgan stated. "Left alone, not have somebody always telling us what we can or can't do," she went on, "and how much of our own money we can keep."

"This **is** America." They all turned to see that Senator Hearst had rejoined them. "Where even an old miner like me can strike pay dirt, and then go to plays, an' ballets, an' fancy eateries, and buy pretty girls Champaign. You girls want some Champaign?" Hearst waved at the bartender who in turn tapped a waiter on the shoulder and pointed at the senator.

"Please sit with us George." Morgan called Hearst by his first name, and he liked that.

"Reckon I'd be obliged to." Hearst pulled an empty chair from another table and scooted it in between Morgan and Stan.

"Short poker night," Morgan quipped with a grin.

"Yup, them boys run outta money in a hurry." The senator chuckled and then added. "The last one bet a night with his wife when he run out. I'd saw that woman already. Got a face that'd make a freight train turn up a dirt road. Told him if'n I won, he had to keep her. I think the sorry bastard really tried to win! Ha, ha. He lost, though! Ha, ha."

The rest at the table joined in with laughter.

"Good evening, Senator," the waiter wearing a white waiter's smock with a cotton napkin draped over his arm greeted Hearst.

"You stickin' with your ale Stan?" The senator asked.

Stan raised his stein in a salute. "Thanks anyway, sir."

"Your best Champaign for the ladies and Jameson. Irish whiskey for me, if you got it."

"Senator Hearst, Miss Morgan, and us too now, think Brower was shot because of his stand on guns. What do you think, sir?" Stan asked.

"Well, it does seem awful suspicious. Every time we get ready for a vote on it, somebody gets plugged full o' holes." Hearst looked over at the bar for the drinks as he spoke. "Yep, mighty suspicious." He turned back to the table. "They don't need to dawdle wit' them drinks." He craned his neck once again at the bar.

"How about that Stryker man," Myrna wanted to know.

"Ain't much I knowed. He's a learned man from back East. Had some trouble there and ended up out West. Morgan here . . .," He caught her short, quick head shake, and stopped. "Said she'd heard he was good at finalizin' things. Kinda like the Army, I guess. Don't want him around too much, though. He gets mud and blood on the carpet–hey!" Hearst yelled to the bartender. "How about them drinks!"

"What's he look like?" Myrna persisted.

"He's a tall man." The senator squirmed back around. "Got eyes you ain't gonna forget, a fierceness in 'em. Might want him wit' me in a fight, wouldn't want ta meet him in the alley."

The waiter rushed to the table with the Champagne and whiskey on a tray, cutting short discussion of the mixed-breed.

CHAPTER SEVEN

Stryker correctly figured the Righteous Sisters would be waiting for him. They'd probably still be there the next day too. He spied the camp fire smoke a mile away. Then the wagon came into view, and lastly humans moving about, eight of them. Eventually one of the Righteous Sisters saw him riding in and waved. He'd held the roan at a walk from Laws because of the damn knife wound, and he fought against digging in his heels now.

He rode on at the same pace. Three hundred yards out; he recognized in addition to the Sisters, a white man with Indians, Paiute probably, their tribe settled Owens Valley. The tribe fought the whites east of the Sierras and lost. Upon returning to the valley, they discovered it'd been taken over white settlers.

When Stryker got within fifty paces, Jemima raced out to meet him.

"I knew you'd come back!" She halted a few feet in front of the roan, beaming a broad smile. "What took so long?" Her puzzled expression morphed to a frown. "We were worried."

"Those people," Stryker demanded, staring at a group of Indians.

"Oh, that's Poenabe and Paya, and some of her tribe. They come by 'bout two hours ago, I guess, on foot. Seem nice. Been talkin' wit 'em."

Jemima reached out to grab the roan's halter. She held it and walked next to the big horse.

Stryker and Jemima didn't speak again until they reached the camp. He swung off the roan and came in beside Jemima.

"Glad you're back, Elvin," Eula said halfheartedly.

"This here's Paya, and he's Poenabe Truckee," Hany said, pointing to each.

Paya smiled politely. A young and striking raven-haired beauty with high cheekbones and blue eyes, she obviously had mixed blood in her. Poenabe, a tall, lanky kid, with long black hair, wearing just a loin-cloth, had a guitar slung on his back. In fact, both Poenabe Truckee and Paya appeared to have come from white parents who'd had Paiute dalliances. Poenabe eyed the fearsome-looking Stryker nervously. The three other Paiutes, a boy and two girls, seemed to be in their teens as well.

"They want something," Stryker said.

Hany couldn't figure out if Stryker made a statement or asked a question. She went with a question. "Uh, no I don't think so. They just wandered in after you left this mornin'."

"More of 'em."

"They said their tribe got moved to Pyramid Lake, a reservation, I guess."

Poenabe Truckee took hold of Paya's arm and crouched, as if preparing to run.

"They wuz tellin' us 'bout themselves," Jemima chimed in. "Her name means 'water' and his is," pointing to the boy, "'Chief'. . . Poenabe means Chief and Truckee means 'everything is all right'–Chief Everything Is All Right."

Chief Everything Is All Right, straightened and beamed proudly. He released Paya's arm.

"The three, his tribe. He's a young chief," Stryker said.

"His papa is the big chief. He guided the settlers up north." Jemima poked out an arm pointing north. "Says they named a big river after 'im, the Truckee River."

Chief Truckee stuck his chest out even more.

"They also tolt 'bout losing their land and their water," Eula said, sounding ominous. "That's why their tribe got moved. But . . ."

"But we're not like the old ones," Paya cut in. "We're the new generation."

Poenabe Truckee and the rest of his small tribe nodded vigorously in agreement.

An awkward silence followed.

It was about that time, the Righteous Sisters, all three, noticed the .44 hanging low off Stryker's right hip. The Peacemaker lurking in its well-used holster wasn't all together lost on the Paiutes either.

"El-vin?" Hany said, raising "vin" to a lofty level. Her eyes locked on the gun.

Stryker drew the Colt with shocking speed. He waved its barrel at Chief Truckee.

"Elvin!" Hany shrieked.

"Truckee, you're about to get religion," Stryker growled.

"What you mean Elvin?" Eula struggled to remain calm.

"Get the outfit."

"Jemima, go get it." Eula quickly understood Stryker's intentions.

"Mister, I don't know what you want from us. We don't have nothin'. Don't mean nothin bad." Poenabe Truckee held out his opened palms. "We got no guns and no knives neither. Can't we just go?" The rest of the young Paiutes, looking fearful, clustered around Paya. They clustered a few feet away from their self-appointed chief, however.

"Here, Stryker." Jemima came from the wagon and held out the garment.

"Give it to him." Stryker waggled the .44 at Truckee. "Put it on, Chief."

"Better put it on, he's killed lots of men," Eula warned Truckee. "You ain't really killed men, have ya?" She asked under her breath as she watched the youngster struggle with the garish garment.

"Mostly assholes, not many men," Stryker growled.

Eula snapped her head around at Stryker. She couldn't tell whether he was serious. He wasn't smiling. She decided he was. A chill went through her. "Who are you?" Her voice trembled.

Truckee handed the guitar to Paya.

"Stryker. He's your new Elvin." Stryker pointed the Colt at the new Elvin. "When he gets that thing on, try one of your songs, a lively one."

Eula hesitated, not sure about what to do.

"Do it now. All of you." Stryker kept the Colt trained on Chief Truckee.

"Hany get the songbook!" Eula clapped her hands rapidly to hurry her sister.

Hany returned with the tattered songbook. "What song we gonna sing Eula?" She handed the book to Eula. Jemima joined them, being careful not to walk between the pointed gun and the chief.

"Here." Paya handed the guitar back to Truckee. She strolled over by the other Paiutes and motioned with her hands for them to sit. They sat. Paya leaned to one, cupped his ear with her hand, and whispered, pointing at their Chief. Both broke into broad grins.

Eula flipped through the songbook and stopped. She placed a forefinger on a page and said, "This one- 'Go Tell It on the Mountain.'" She looked up from the book and at Truckee. "Can you play that?" meaning the guitar.

"Yeah, some."

"Come over here and play it then." Stryker's Peacemaker aided Eula's authority.

Chief Truckee moved hesitantly to stand next to the Righteous Sisters. "Can you hum a little of it, first? I think I hear'd it before, but . . . I"

Eula broke in humming a few notes before he could finish.

Stryker holstered the Peacemaker.

"Okay, here we go." And Eula started off with the first line. *"Go tell it on the mountain, over the hills and everywhere. . ."* Hany and Jemima joined in. *"Go tell it on the mountain, that Jesus Christ is born. . ."* By the time they got to the next verse, Truckee began to gingerly strum the chords.

"Wait. Hold it." Eula interrupted. "We can't hardly hear ya Chief. Let's start over."

Chief Truckee dropped his hands from the guitar, shook them as if flinging water off, and then locked them together to flex. He straightened his arms, reversing the palms outward, and vigorously stretched his fingers. "The Poenabe is ready." He spread his legs, readied his hands on the guitar, and in one loud down stroke of his thumb on the strings . . . became Elvin.

This time when the Righteous Sisters sang, Elvin played. And oh, how he played-shaking, writhing, hips thrusting, legs moving every which way.

"My goodness Elvin!" Eula exclaimed when the song was completed. "We had Holy Rollers rolling on the floor in Georgia, and the choir, they all rocked them bodies with the music but thaz was nuthin' like what you a doin' boy. What you got a going on in them pants Elvin?" She called him Elvin. "Looks like all kinds a hell breakin' loose in there."

Paya and the Paiutes, shocked at first, began to applaud, slowly at first, and then loudly with a lot of shouting.

"Why, I don't know, ma'am. The music, this outfit, they just gets me goin'." Chief Elvin looked apologetic. "But I like it. I like the music . . . I like this outfit!" He held the guitar out away from his body and surveyed his get up. "Rollin' and rockin'. Roll and Rock!"

"What you think, mister?" Stryker was no longer Elvin to Eula.

"You're close Elvin, real close, but you're on to something big. Roll and Rock, yep, something really big."

The Righteous Sisters and the Paiutes gathered around the new Elvin, all talking at the same time. They failed to notice Stryker swinging back up on the roan and turning it toward Bishop Creek.

By the time Stryker rode in town from the north, the sun sat atop the Sierra Nevada's. Bishop Creek appeared more alive than Laws. It seemed to gain what Laws was losing, and not just people. It boasted new buildings with fresh paint, flowers, trees, and bustled with activity. At the north end of town, the bright yellow sign with white lettering read "Bishop Creek Pop. 300." Unlike Laws, Bishop Creek catered to ranching instead of mining. Samuel Bishop established a ranch two miles west in 1861, and the town, Bishop Creek, sprung up east of the ranch. A little brook flowed south, murmuring through a lush meadow where the town nested. Fremont cottonwoods, various types of willows, and shrub trees grew abundantly along Main Street running parallel to the creek. The banner stretching across Main Street read *"Revival–August 1 thru August 4."* Stryker rode under it and passed by Bishop Creek Hotel on his left, opting not to stop there. Too much noise, and too many people. Farther down, at the south end of town, he saw Adam's Livery. Better secure a room first. He reined in the roan by Stella's Boarding House.

Stella, a stout woman, who apparently loved her own cooking, if her ample girth was an indication, welcomed the mixed-breed into the two-story inn. Decorated cheerfully with colorful wallpaper and fresh flowers in a vase on the entryway table, the place almost brightened Stryker's mood. Seeing her newest arrival as none too friendly, Stella held back at first. However, she forced a broad smile that pushed up her rosy cheeks.

"Welcome, Mister . . .," Stella paused for a name.

"Stryker."

"Will you be staying just one night or longer?" Stella quickly added, "It's cheaper by the week."

"More than a day."

"Uh, well, the weekly rate then, dollar-fifty a night, twelve for the week."

Stryker let it slide. He hoped the cooking was better than her math. "All right."

"Upstairs, last room on the left. C'mon in, we're just sitting down for supper." Stella waived a meaty arm at the arched doorway on her left.

Four men already seated at the table, eating meatloaf and mashed potatoes, stopped talking when Stryker entered the room. Three of the men, a gruff-looking bunch, took a cue to end the conversation from the fourth man, Councilman Eddie Ralston. Nervous glances exchanged between the four men. Ralston took it upon himself to address the new guest who scraped back a chair from the table. The other three returned to eating.

It took a while. The new man looked threatening. The councilman let Stryker down a mouthful of meatloaf first. "My name's Edward Ralston, mister. I'm a councilman here and I was just getting to know these other fellows. You're new in Bishop Creek, are ya?"

Stryker nodded as he stuck another piece the meatloaf in his mouth. Ralston glanced at the other three and signaled them with a slight head shake to play along.

Stryker reached for more meatloaf.

"Yeah, so are them." Ralston jabbed an empty fork at the other three men. "This here's Ashe, and he's Texas. What d'you say your name was?" Ralston already knew the third man, though.

"R.J." R.J. looked puzzled. "Uh, pass them potatoes."

Ralston returned to Stryker, "You visit'n for a while or pass'n through? I might could help some if I know'd your business." Ralston already overheard Stryker say he'd be in town for more than a day. He fished for what Stryker was doing in Bishop Creek.

Stryker re-filled his coffee cup.

The councilman held his anger at being ignored. He glanced at Ashe, the biggest of the three men. Ashe had a clump of potato stuck in his scraggly beard. It jiggled when he chewed. He stopped chewing, carefully set his fork beside his plate, and brought his hands beneath the table. He readied himself for Ralston to give the order. It didn't happen, and he continued jiggling the potato clump.

Stryker swilled the last of the coffee in his cup, didn't wait for the apple pie sitting on the serving table, and got to his feet. He walked from the dining room and went outside to the roan.

Ralston thought about inquiring more, but the .44 on Stryker's hip quelled his curiosity. The gun belt and holster had seen better days, but the Colt looked prime, well cared for, and well used. The councilman reloaded potatoes on his fork, "I don't like this fellow. Comin' in ta' town is one thing, staying on is another. Watch him. See who he talks to. Find out what he wants." Ralston wiped his mouth with a napkin. "Tex, why don't you go have a smoke on the porch." He said, directing a crooked grin at the Texan. "Might as well start now."

Texas rose from the table. Outside, he pulled the makin's from his shirt pocket, looked right, then left, and saw Stryker with the roan, entering the livery. A light drizzle began, the kind without raindrops, but everything gets wet anyway. The Texan lit the rolled cigarette and stepped off the porch. He made his way down the side alley and took a back street toward the stable.

Stryker slid open the large hanging door to the stable and led the roan inside. Light was poor, and he had to allow a few minutes for his eyes to adjust. A flat pull-cart piled high with horse manure set parked two-thirds down the center corridor. Being freshly shoveled, the turds lay cracked open. Their odor blended with the heavy smell of metal oxides still hanging about the forge. At first, he thought the livery deserted since no one tended the forge. The fire barely glowed. But he heard someone sweeping a stall at the far end. He looped the reins over a top rail and started along the corridor. He'd only gone halfway when the kid stepped out from a stall, carrying a shovel of manure.

"Aaahhh! Shit! You scared me, mister. Didn't hear ya come in." The boy appeared to be around fourteen years old, tall and gangly. Already missing front teeth and sporting a bumper crop of pimples, he probably didn't have too many girls sneaking into the livery to give him a kiss.

"Got a horse to stable," Stryker said.

"Fifty cents a day. Seventy-five with feed and curry." The boy dumped the shovel's contents on the cart and stuck the blade in the greenish pile of turds. "That him?" he nodded toward the roan.

"Curry and feed. Might be a few days. Needing information too."

The kid had passed Stryker on his way to the roan, but stopped and turned around to face the mixed-breed. "Yes, sir?"

"The biggest outfits around here, ranching, farming."

"That'd be the Cavin spread for sure, if you're looking for cattle. He's south and west, 'bout ten miles I guess. You might go ask at Cina's Hardware and Emporium. Steph Cina knows just about ever' body in the valley. Main street, on the left."

Stryker fished five silver dollars from his pocket. "Here. And no one knows my business." He dropped the silver in the kid's hand.

The youngster stared at the money. He stuffed the coins in his pocket and said, "Yes sir. My name's Dillan if'n you need somethin' more."

Stryker walked out of the livery. As he came outside, a quick movement on his right caught his eye. A man darted out from sight around the corner of the building adjacent to the livery. Suspicious, Stryker whirled left, opposite the sighting, and moved along the front of the stable. He drew the Peacemaker and waited at the corner's edge. No one showed. He slowly made his way down the side of building, stepping quietly alongside the rough-hewn boards. At the back of the livery, he stopped again. The heavy door to the stable hung open, and he could hear a man grunting gruff demands. With each mumbling response, he heard a punch, like a fist to a face. Then another question asked, one more demanding. Stryker couldn't make out their words. He inched closer to the door.

"Don't tell me he didn't say nothin'." A grunt, a punch, a moan. "Wha'd he say? Who's he meetin'?" A grunt, a punch, a moan. "Water, he askin' 'bout water?" Grunt, punch, but no moan. "God dammit–hey! Wake up kid. Shit. Shi-t! All right pimple face. I'll be back, an' next time I won't go so easy on ya."

Stryker heard a boot kick to the body. Probably to the face. He holstered the Colt, reached behind for the sai, and flipped it upside down along his forearm. He dropped to a crouch.

Texas stepped through the door and came face to face with Stryker. Stryker sprang forward, driving the sai handle into the man's forehead. It struck Texan's forehead with a sickening thunk, and he stumbled back inside the livery.

Stryker leaped on him. Gripping Texas's throat, he pinned his neck against a post. Stryker whirled the sai and shoved the center tine up the man's nose. Stryker glanced down and saw Dillon on the floor, his battered face lying in a pool of blood.

"Now, I have questions," Stryker growled.

The eyes of the Texan glazed over. Stryker jiggled the sai.

"Who gives orders?" Stryker demanded.

Texas clamped his mouth closed. Stryker jiggled the sai again.

"Ralston," Texas croaked weakly. The pain intensified. His eyes began to tear, and he screwed them shut.

"Who else?"

"Werner, L.A. Water Commish . . . gonna kill you for this." Texas rasped.

Stryker dropped lower. He locked the sai arm to his shoulder, and lunged upward.

Texas's eyes burst open and went blank as the tine punctured his brain. Stryker yanked the sai from his nostril, and Texas crumbled to the dirt. His face landed on a pile of horseshit.

Stryker decided to pay a visit to the Cavin man and walked out the rear entrance. He left Dillon, who'd earned his pay, lying beside the body of the dead Texan. The blacksmith returned later that night and found both still on the stable floor in the dirt and horse shit. The boy revived. Texas refused to stir.

"What the hell did you do to 'im?" The livery man asked, as he knelt by the corpse. A large amount of dried blood caked the dirt and horse shit by the dead man's face.

"Nothun'. Last I 'membered, he wuz poundin' the shit outta me. Is he dead?" Dillon mumbled the words with a bloody mouth and broken teeth.

"He shore acts like it."

"I didn't kill 'im. Honest." Dillon sat up sharply. Spraying blood through missing teeth, he said, "I never touched 'im, Wagner!" He looked scared.

"Wouldn't blame ya if you did, boy. You took a beatin' son." Wagner lifted Texas's chin to get a better look at the man's face. "He shore bled a lot. I reckon he wore his-self out on you, boy. Had a stroke or somethun'. He don't appear hurt none, ain't no marks on him."

At first Dillon figured the blacksmith was right. But he wondered if the mean-looking fellow who'd been in earlier had returned. He never mentioned that to anybody.

Stryker headed to a saloon he'd passed earlier, *Galt's Gulp Saloon*. It was farther up the main street, on the other side from Stella's. He wasn't particularly thirsty, but he figured to sip a beer and keep his ears open. After a quick scan of the bar room over the bat-wing doors, he pushed them open. A single-story building with a low metal ceiling, the saloon kept the cigar smoke tightly confined. The bar counter ran along the right side of the room. Behind the bar, a wide painting of a young woman, wearing chaps and naked from the waist up, sat on a long-horn bull. She looked fetching. Tables and chairs sat opposite the bar. At the far end, a barber's chair rested by the back wall. It seemed as if it had been plucked, or stolen, from a barber shop and placed there on display. Stryker thought it looked regal. On his left, a long mirror, roughly three feet high, hung on the wall across from the bare-breasted bull rider, so cowboys could reflect on her charms. A couple of poker players glanced his way and went back to the cards they held. Satisfied he garnered no unusual attention, Stryker walked over to the bar. Two other men talking and drinking whiskey at the counter, scooted a little farther down to give him room, perhaps keeping their conversations to themselves.

"What'll it be, mister?" Asked the bartender dressed like a barber, wearing a black bow tie, arm garters, shirt and vest, and an apron.

"Beer."

The bar-keep poured a full mug and slapped it on the counter, slopping foam down the glass. "Two bits. Make it a dollar, mister. Get a cut and shave with it."

Stryker bounced the coin on the bar and lifted the glass. He blew off more of the foam and sipped the beer. "Beer'll do." He turned away from the bar, leaned back against it, and propped both elbows on the counter. Ranchers or cow hands, farmers too, he figured, sat at the tables drinking, and talking in low tones, except when the cards weren't friendly. There were maybe thirteen or fourteen. All of them looked like regulars, and none seemed interested in him. He took two more swallows and strolled over to the barber chair.

Outside, a distant drumbeat wafted above the bat wings. As it grew closer, Stryker heard the jangle of a tambourine as well. The pounding and clanging got louder and louder until the racket was outside the saloon. Then it stopped. A tall, thin, man with a long beard, in a black preacher's suit burst through the bat wings. He stood erect and sanctimonious, holding the Bible against his chest.

"Holy shit!" A card player exclaimed.

"Yep, shore is," added another.

Three women in bonnets and long dresses, also toting Bibles, filed in behind the preacher. The tambourine lady crowded in with the drummer woman. Thankfully, two women did not play their instruments. And finally, Elvin and the Righteous Sisters pushed inside. Elvin wore his outfit.

"There's a revival tonight!" the preacher thundered. "And all you men of the wayward flock need to be there!" He pointed and stabbed a bony forefinger finger around the room. His attention lingered a bit on the bull rider.

"Sir -," the barkeeper began.

"Six o'clock!" The preacher got back to soul saving. "In the big tent at the -," He turned to the three women and whispered, "Is that north or south of town?"

"East, I think," answered one.

"Edge of town!"

The livery, located at the south end of Bishop Creek, allowed Stryker to ride out for the Cavin ranch without going through town again. He rode due south for three miles and came to a well-used trail that forked off to the southeast. He took it, and within another mile or so he came to the banks of the Owen River. After allowing the roan to suck a few gulps of the cool water, he forded the river and continued south. Presently, he spotted clumps of cattle grazing in the lush grass along the river and figured they must be Cavin stock. Riding closer, the herd grew larger, and he saw the "Rocking C" brand on their flanks. Another eight miles, and Stryker spied what seemed like an outline of a town. It turned out to be Cavin's ranch. There was the main house, two casitas, a barn, or barns, one for hay and one for equipment, a long stable, multiple tool sheds, and three one-story ranch houses in a row for the hired hands. The back half of the main three-story house towered high enough so a person standing on the upper balcony could see out over the barns and have an unobstructed view in any direction. Cavin had done pretty well for himself.

Stryker stayed on the trail until he came to a twelve-foot adobe arch with "Cavin," in big rustic iron letters across the top. Beyond it, a flagstone lane lined with cottonwoods on both sides curled up to the main house. He wheeled the roan left and rode under the arch. The lane must have been at least a quarter mile long. The roan's shod hoofs clopping on the flagstone announced his coming, and Stryker figured the flagstone wasn't just for looks.

As Stryker rode up to within a hundred paces, a tall cowboy in chaps with a double-barrel shotgun resting in the crook of his elbow came out onto the porch. When Stryker reined the roan to a halt in front of the brightly colored veranda, the shotgun was swung his way.

"What's your business, mister?" The rail thin cowboy with a weathered face kept the barrels pointed at Stryker. From where Stryker sat, he could tell the hammers remained forward.

"See a man called Cavin." Stryker crossed his arms and leaned forward, resting them on the saddle horn.

"Reckon I knowed that. What you want with him?" The cowboy didn't like the looks of Stryker. He thought about cocking the shotgun.

"Between me an' him."

"If'n you don't . . ."

"Hold on Rex." The front door swung open. "I'm Cavin."

Stryker straightened and swung from the roan. He tied the reins a rail by the porch. "Water problem."

"If you've come to buy my water, you can just climb back on the horse." Cavin, a big strapping man well over six feet tall, came out to stand beside Rex.

Rex cocked the shotgun.

"Keep your water."

Cavin eyed Stryker for a bit before asking. "Who sent you?"

"Put the shotgun away."

Rex glanced over to his boss. Cavin nodded his head. Rex pointed the shotgun off to the side and eased both hammers forward.

"All right, mister. What's on your mind? And I wanna know who sent you." Cavin wasn't dropping his guard.

"Can't tell you who sent me. I'm here to make sure you keep what's yours. That includes water," Stryker said flatly.

Cavin and Stryker stared at each other for what seemed like a full minute. Rex caressed the shotgun hammers with his thumb, but didn't cock them.

"Come inside and let's talk." Cavin turned and went in the house.

Rex caught the door before it closed and held it open, "After you, mister."

"Cavin stood across the spacious front room, pouring a drink of labeled whiskey at a mahogany wood bar topped with hand-tooled leather. He kept his back to Stryker as he filled the glass half full with whiskey. Stryker inspected the impressive room, furnished with man-sized padded, leather chairs, several pieces of artwork on the walls and tables, and cowhide rugs on the polished Saltillo tile. Without facing his guest, he asked, "You want a drink?"

"Yeah."

When Cavin turned with two drinks in hand, he saw Stryker had already settled into a chair. He handed a glass to Stryker and sat across from him.

Even sitting, Cavin looked imposing. His broad shoulders hid the chair back, and his muscular arms suggested he'd thrown more than a few calves to the ground. He wore a full head of hair closely cropped on the sides and bushy on top. A stern and wrinkled brow indicated long work days.

"William, my friends call me Bill," Cavin said, and he drank a mouthful of the whiskey. What do yours call you?"

"Name's Stryker."

"Stryker, tell me again why I should trust you."

"There's a man from Los Angeles called Werner, and another named Ralston."

"Ralston, he's on the town council, and Werner? Yeah, that bastard is from Los Angeles. What about 'em?" Cavin asked.

"They've hired some toughs, maybe for persuading men like you." Stryker tested the whiskey.

"Hmmm, how many?"

"Ran into three of 'em. There's two now. Don't know if there's more than that."

It didn't take much for Cavin to conclude the fellow sitting across from him had something to do with the missing man.

"Well Stryker, how much do you know about the water here?"

"You have it. They want it."

"That's right, and I heard they want to build an irrigation system for the ranchers and farmers in Owens valley. That's bullshit. I run ten-thousand head of cattle on my ranch, started with fifty of 'em sixteen years ago. Got plenty of water for 'em now. Don't need their help." Cavin slowly turned the glass in his big hand. "I want to show you somethun'. Take you for a ride south o' here. Be two or three days. Had a couple wranglers come up from Lone Pine way. Saw something I wanna take a look at. Said they got shot at and couldn't get close enough to see good. We leave in the morning if you're up for it."

"I—," Stryker started.

"He'll be glad to, and he'll stay the night."

Stryker twisted in the chair to see a stern-faced woman in her mid-forties. Her stern countenance more than made up for her small stature. She pushed a wheelchair, with a girl in it, slumped to one side, dozing.

"Let's not be rude, Bill." A warm smile fractured the austere expression, and she flashed a playful twinkle in her eyes. And when she did that, she became more attractive.

Who rules this nest? Stryker mused to himself.

"My wife, Elizabeth," Cavin grumbled. "The girl in the chair is Susan, Susan Peters, my niece. She's come to stay with us for a while." The girl, perhaps in her mid-to-late twenties, was a frail and fragile figure with a gentle, pretty face in repose. "She had a gun accident a few years ago that left her with a bullet lodged in her spine."

Susan, upon hearing her name, stirred in the chair. Her eyes flitted several times, attempting to focus on the new house guest. The girl's bones poked through her skin, especially the cheekbones. Her eyes were dark and sunken. The corner of her mouth twitched, as if struggling to force a grin, but the effort had no energy. She sat, staring blankly at Stryker.

"Paralyzed from the waist down," Cavin said to Stryker. "Susan honey, this is Mister Stryker." Cavin lifted his glass toward Stryker. He'll be with us for a few days. Gonna show him around some in the morning. How you feelin'?"

Elizabeth answered for Susan. "She's had a rough day."

Stryker and the girl locked eyes. Their gaze remained fixed until Elizabeth, somewhat awkwardly, broke in. "Uh, have you, uh, met before?"

Susan shook her head no, but still stared at Stryker. For the first time since the bullet lodged in her back, she sensed here was a man who somehow understood her loss, her pain. Her husband hadn't. He ran off after the gun accident. Maybe she ran him off. She could be bitchy. She was mad at the world and everyone in it. And she hurt all the time. In constant pain, Susan got no relief, awake or asleep. In fact, she seldom slept more than a few minutes at a time. Paralyzed from the waist down, but the loss of feeling did not extend to the fiery cords which ran down her butt and legs. The pain became her constant companion, her only companion. It never left her. She even named it. Called it Joe.

Susan never knew a Joe. Perhaps the name being a single syllable was enough. And she could say it through gritted teeth.

She attempted another smile. Some of it fought through to show on her face.

Stryker dipped his head.

"Fernando should have supper about ready, Bill." Elizabeth interjected. "You hungry, Mister Stryker?" she asked.

"Reckon so, ma'am."

The Cavins served supper in a room away from the more formal front room. Not exactly a separate area, more like a spacious alcove between where they had been sitting and talking, and the kitchen. The long solid oak table usually accommodated twelve. William and Elizabeth assumed their chairs at the ends, allowing Stryker and Susan together at the middle with a view out over the open veranda.

"You fancy steak, Stryker?" Without waiting for a reply, Cavin continued, "Cause if you do, you're about to have a cut of the best beef west of Texas."

When the steaks and baked potatoes with creamed corn were brought, three people cut into their medium-rare filets. Susan stared at hers.

Elizabeth implored her husband to do something with a facial plea.

Cavin shook his head no, gesturing frustration.

"You can include Texas," Stryker said, slicing off another chunk of steak.

"Want to ride that roan of yours or one of mine? Leavin' at first light." Cavin shifted his gaze from Elizabeth to Stryker.

"Ride my own."

"All right, I'll have a man walk him down to the stable. He'll have a good night's rest, sponge, curry, feed and water. Bring him up in the morning. Liz will show you to your room. Need anything off the horse?"

"I'll get it." Stryker took one last forkful and scooted from the table.

"That man kinda reminds me of somebody, wish I could remember." Cavin's gazed at Stryker's empty chair.

"You've maybe seen him before?" Elizabeth offered.

"Could've, not any time recent."

The following morning a few straggling stars hung in the sky to greet Stryker and Cavin stepping off the front porch. The roan and Cavin's sorrel stood hitched to the front rail, saddled with full canteens, plus hardtack, biscuits, and beans in the saddlebags. The two men rode five miles, heading southeast when the sun yawned over the snow-capped White Mountains. Sunlight crawled down from the peaks of the Sierra's to the west. Neither man spoke much as they rode the trail along the Owens River.

They stopped in Big Pine to rest and water the horses. It was only after Big Pine that Bill wandered into a conversation. "Came out to California after the War. I miss Texas sometimes, but guess I needed to make a new start, get as far away from that damned War as I could." He got no response from the mixed-breed, but he went on anyway. "Reckon you're too young for to be in it. I—,"

"I was in it."

Cavin swung attention from between his horse's ear to Stryker. "North, South?"

"North."

"Well, I reckon it don't matter now. Hell, best I can recall, seemed like we just chose up sides and started killing each other." Cavin rolled up saliva to spit, leaning off the sorrel opposite Stryker. "I fought for the South cause Texas is in the south. You know something Stryker, if all the men in the south switched places with all the men in the north, all of us would have worn blue and all of you boys woulda worn gray. We just fought for our side, never really knowing why. Them higher ups, like them damn politicians, said it was slavery, or eeco-nomics, or something else they got all riled up over. But we-uns done the bleeding and dying for honor and home. I often wonder what would've happened if we hadn't gone to war. It probably woulda worked out. Now don't get me wrong, there's some things to fight for, freedom for one, but that fucking war killed 600,000-700,000 of us, and what got done? Machines was doing more and more field work, and it was costing more and more to keep them poor wretches than they was worth. Anyway, I got knocked outta the fight'n in '62. Antietam–you any part of that one, Stryker? Naw, you was too young, I reckon."

"North called it Sharpsburg. Yeah, I was there."

"You musta been awful—there *wuz* a lot kids fightin'."

"Fifteen, maybe, didn't matter. Boys grew up fast then."

"Infantry?"

"Artillery, 20-pound Parrott rifle." Stryker replied. The last couple of words drifted out.

Cavin turned in the saddle, studying Stryker. The cornfield—you on one of them cannons. That's where I see'd you before." Cavin remained staring at Stryker and continued. "Shit. Yeah, you wuz jus' a youngin' all right, but no mistakin' them eyes you got. You almost got me, Stryker."

Stryker swung in the saddle and looked at Cavin riding beside him. He scrunched his eyebrows, trying to remember Bill.

Cavin helped him. "I'd already took a bullet. Hit me in the chest, knocked me down. Got back up to my knees. Us boys from the 1st Texas charged through that corn, almost made to them guns–thirty feet, I reckin'." Cavin faced forward now, looking at the trail ahead as he spoke. "It wuz pure hell. We-all got slaughtered. Bullets flying all over. My God, they wuz thick–cut corn to the ground. Jesus." Cavin paused, took a deep breath, and his voice dropped lower. "I don't see how we got that close. I think I's the only one left standin', and I wuz on my knees. I jus' kept a kneelin'on 'em, staring at the mouth of that big gun, waitin' for it to blow a hole in me."

Cavin looked at Stryker. "That's where I saw you. You wuz gonna fire it."

CHAPTER EIGHT

The cornfield.

David R. Miller looked forward to harvesting the corn he'd raised on his 24 acres that September 17, 1862. Another couple of weeks and the hair on the corncobs would be entirely brown, telling Miller it was time to pick the corn. Rain fell during the night, and a heavy mist hung in the moist air as dawn broke in the morning. The stalks stood tall, glistening with beads of raindrops on their leaves.

Artillery fire instead of roosters announced the start of a new day.

Rifles, canteens, and equipment rattled on thousands of troops marching in the woods surrounding the field. Officers barked commands to subordinates. All the troops remained out of sight in the forest. Not being able to see them made their presence seem more ominous. There was to be an enormous clash.

General Lee brought 15,000 Confederate troops for a raid into Maryland. General McClellan had 60,000 Union soldiers to stop him. They chose Miller's cornfield to do battle. Blue attacked from the north, gray from the south. For nearly four hours they pushed each other back and forth through the corn, until there was no more corn. The assault on the senses was stupefying. The cacophonous din from the guns and cannons drove some men senseless. A commonly used phrase, *the fog of war,* accurately described the furious fighting. Lead filled the air. It seemed to make the gun smoke and mist too heavy to rise from the ground. Men moved like apparitions, appearing and disappearing through the thick fog. Their eyes were starkly white on faces blackened with gunpowder. But the eyes were ringed in red, brought on by stress and fatigue. The acrid smell of burnt powder, congealed blood, and loosened bowels invaded the nostrils. Driven by an indomitable will to live, soldiers dragged bodies with missing limbs, crawling without purpose except in a vain attempt to escape the hell they were in–until they died. Traumatized by horrific injuries many soldiers died from shock. And from that dark veil of death came the screaming, crying, and praying of desperate men who lay dying. Men and boys alike begged for God or their mamas to please help them.

Stryker was alone on the cannon. Except for Sergeant Walters, the rest of the eight-man crew lay dead around the Parrott rifle. Corporal Jenkins had stopped moaning fifteen minutes before. The Sergeant still clung to life. He had bullets in both legs, one in his stomach, and another lodged near his collarbone. It came to rest there after smashing through his mouth as he picked up a 20-pound shell. Walters lay propped up on an elbow, still giving orders. His jaws flapped as he yelled, the words flowing out of his mouth on blood. His loud, muffled barking of commands would have been comical, if he weren't dying.

Stryker couldn't understand the Sergeant's commands. It didn't matter. He knew how to set and ram the charge down the front of the muzzle. He'd been on the gun crew four months. Swarms of bullets pinged on the cannon barrel, ricocheting off to tear through his coat sleeves. He threw the shell down the bore. No need to sight the gun. It was already leveled. Just load it and fire it across the cornfield, point blank.

"Fire it boy!" Sergeant Walters yelled the order in bloody bubbles. Those were the Sergeant's final words. He settled back off his elbow and died.

Stryker ran around the gun to the breech, reset the primer, and grabbed the lanyard. He paused for a half second. Did he do it right? He jerked the rope.

The gun exploded—at the breech block. The blast blew Stryker off his feet, sending him somersaulting him ten feet away. The Parrett rifle, notorious for exploding after heavy firing, had blown up.

Stryker came to several hours later, long after the fighting had ceased. He rose to his feet and wobbled to the rear lines by Dunker Church.

Corporal Cavin saw it all. Then as he swayed there, wavering, ready to topple off his knees, someone grabbed him from behind, and lifted him to his feet. Half carrying, half dragging, a fellow Texan got him up and out of the cornfield.

Farmer Miller lost his crop that day, a day still remembered as the bloodiest battle in American history with 20,000 casualties.

"All I remember now is the gun blew up. I thought it kilt you, and I wuz glad." Cavin glanced at Stryker. "But that was back then, and thank God we're both alive today."

Stryker nodded his head.

"Stryker, aside from this water business, I might have a favor to ask," Cavin said. "Talk about it later."

Four hours later and roughly sixteen miles south of Big Pine, Cavin reined the sorrel off the trail, crossed the Owens River, and started up a hill. Stryker followed as the rancher picked his way up through ancient lava rock, deposited there from volcanic activity tens of thousands of years ago. Once the two riders crested the plateau, Cavin dismounted and pulled field glasses out of his saddlebag. He climbed onto one of the larger pieces of the black lava, flat and smooth, and sat. Drawing up his knees, he propped his elbows on top to steady the binoculars. Cavin viewed through them for the better part of a minute and handed the glasses to Stryker who'd joined him on the rock. "Here, take a look down yonder," he said, pointing at men laboring in a wide ditch, a quarter mile distant. "What you think is going on down there?"

Stryker took the binoculars, refocused them, and sighted in on the workers swinging picks and shoveling dirt. He handed the field glasses back, and before he could reply, Cavin said, "Looks to me like them boys are digging a canal or–."

"Aqueduct." Stryker interrupted.

"Yeah, an aqueduct," Cavin repeated. "Where you suppose they'll get the water to fill it?"

Stryker pulled out the Peacemaker, half-cocked it, and rotated the cylinder, methodically clicking it six times as he eyed each chamber. He slid the Colt back in the holster. "Let's go ask 'em."

"Why not?" Cavin lifted his revolver a couple inches and jammed it back in the holster.

They re-mounted at the bottom of the hill and rode abreast toward the fifty, or so, men working the ditch. As the two men approached, they heard pickaxes stabbing the ground peppered with stones, shovels digging in the dirt, and grunts from the workers. Over half of the laborers were Europeans, the rest, Mexicans and Indians. White men did the grunting. Mexicans and Indians toiled silently. Up close, Cavin and Stryker saw the angular shape of a canal, expanding in a straight line some thirty feet wide and ten feet deep. Perhaps nearing a quarter mile in length, it still had two hundred miles to reach Los Angeles. Ten or twelve open bed wagons stood empty nearby. Stryker suspected the men were housed farther south and hauled up daily from Lone Pine.

Off to the west roughly three hundred paces, Stryker saw a green tarp sheltering seven men from the hot sun, sitting and standing around field tables studying maps or blueprints. Three black buggies still harnessed to horses waited on the south side of the tent. One man looked up and saw Cavin and Stryker. He elbowed another and pointed in their direction. Three men emerged from the tent and walked toward the visitors. Stryker noticed one of them carried a shotgun, a double-barreled shotgun.

Four men remained behind, standing under the edge of the tarp, watching the three walk through the knee-high grass. Were they expecting a confrontation? They sure acted like it.

Stryker let them get within twenty paces before he dismounted. Cavin swung from the sorrel as well.

"Help you fellows?" The tall, muscular man wearing khaki trousers and a matching shirt asked. He stopped ten away; feet spread shoulder width apart, hands on hips. He wore a tan fedora with a maroon bandana tied around his neck. The top of the shirt lay open, showing the scarf ends drooping down a tan chest. The man on his right, a head shorter, wearing the same style khakis but with no scarf and no open collar, wore the countenance on his clean-shaven face of a follower–a sly, sneaky, little prick. His eyes jumped nervously back and forth between Cavin and Stryker and the tall man beside him. He acted as if waiting for someone else to act while he watched and stayed out of it. The shotgun toter was no civil engineer. He carried the weapon in both hands, leveled but not pointed at Cavin or Stryker, not yet anyway. His firm jaw was unshaven. He had the squinty eyes and the hardened face of a violent man. He kept his squinty eyes on Stryker only.

"Looks like you're digging a canal," Cavin drawled in his Texas accent.

The scarf wearer glanced right and then left at his companions. Using half a lip for a smile, he sneered, "That's right." He shifted his eyes from Cavin to Stryker and the half-smile slunk away.

Cavin stared hard at the man doing the talking. "What you gonna fill it with?"

"Jelly."

The wannabe snickered and then cut it short when neither Cavin nor Stryker displayed humor.

"You ain't comin' up here and takin' our water," Cavin warned.

"Who are you two? Excuse me. My name's Campbell, Marion Campbell. I'm in charge here." He nodded sideways at the shorter man to his right. "Ricky Roe." Campbell hooked a thumb to his left. "He's Mike, helps with . . . let's just say he's handy in disagreements."

"I'll say it again, Campbell. Go back to Los Angeles. You ain't gettin' the water." Cavin turned to Stryker. "C'mon, let's go."

Both men had swiveled around toward the horses when Campbell said, "Mike kill–" Campbell failed to complete the order.

Stryker spun, drew, and fired. The .44 slug smashed into Mike's chest rocking him on his heels. He struggled mightily to point the shotgun. His thumb fumbled weakly on the hammers. Stryker fired again. The second round ended Mike's effort. He met his maker before hitting the ground.

Stryker trained the Colt on Campbell's chest, left of center, and pulled the trigger. One bullet was enough. He simply crumbled to the dirt without a sound.

Roe threw both hands high. "Don't shoot! I'm not with . . . I'll go." He hurriedly rattled off the nervous pleading. "Just let me . . ." The Peacemaker barked a fourth time. "Leave," Roe groaned." And he went. Rather, his spirit went, wherever spirits of weasels like him go.

Stryker bent down, threw a two-dollar gold piece on Mike's chest, and picked up the shotgun. Holding it jammed between his upper arm and body, he ejected four shells from the Colt and dug bullets from his gun belt to refill the cylinders. "Tell those men in the ditch the job's finished. Leave and don't come back." He holstered the Colt and shifted the shotgun to his right hand, holding it by the grip, barrel pointing down. He started for the tent.

By the time Stryker walked halfway to the tarp, the four men had turned and scrambled for the buggies. They tore off in two. Stryker strolled to the remaining buggy, turned the horse toward the work wagons, and struck the horse's ass with the buggy whip. Under the tent he looked over the blueprints and maps on the tables. He rolled three of the blueprints and two maps and stuck them under his arm. Walking up to the three dead men and their four bullets, Stryker broke open the shotgun and pulled out the shells. After throwing the shells in a nearby creek, he laid the gun propped against Mike's body. He retrieved his coin and joined Cavin at the horses. Stryker noticed the workmen had climbed out of the canal and were hurriedly throwing tools in the wagons. Stryker secured the papers behind his saddle with rawhide straps and mounted the roan. Cavin climbed on the sorrel, and the two men started back north.

"That feller ain't gonna need the gun, Stryker," Cavin said, wondering why Stryker returned the shotgun to a dead man. The Texan would go on wondering. The mixed-breed never gave a reason why he did it. In fact, there were a lot of questions about the man that went unanswered.

After a half hour's ride, Cavin broke the silence. "There's gonna be a ruckus over them men you just killed." Upon waiting several minutes for a reply, which never came, he added, "Did you have to kill them other two?"

"No."

Cavin weighed Stryker's answer for a good stretch. "Well, I reckon I owe you for saving my life. Kinda evens things up, I guess. But I will ask that favor." After another long pause, he added, "You're damn quick with that gun."

It was getting late when Cavin and Stryker rode into Big Pine, and they spent the night in Maude's Boarding House. Maude, who could have been a Russian potato farmer before moving to Big Pine, cooked huge meals with a lot of lard. Much to the relief of the roan and sorrel, both men made lengthy visits to the small house in back, prior to saddling up the next morning.

Later in the day they rode past growing herds of Cavin's cattle. Realizing he hadn't said anything for over an hour, Cavin said, "A lot of steak on them hooves, Stryker. You hungry?"

"How was your trip?" Elizabeth asked, when Stryker and her husband came through the door later the same day.

"Just as I suspected," Cavin huffed, throwing his Stetson on the entry table by the door. "They're building an aqueduct."

"Aqueduct?" Elizabeth glanced at Stryker. "You mean like for water? To where?" She came back to Cavin.

"Los Angeles. They're aiming to take our water, Liz, and run it down to Los Angeles."

"Why, that's over two hundred miles, Bill. How would it . . .?"

"Gravity," Stryker interjected. "Four thousand feet up here to three hundred down there."

"What are we gonna do?" Elizabeth motioned for the men to come in the living room. "Sit down. You must be thirsty." She waved at the Mexican maid standing by the kitchen door. "Bring us some cold water, Miranda."

"We stopped the digging for now. Uh, Stryker stopped it," Cavin said as both men sat. "They'll be back, though. Bringing guards, I reckon, when they do."

"Oh no, you mean fighting with guns?" Elizabeth asked, scrunching her face to show her displeasure with gunplay.

"We'll try it legal first," Cavin answered, assuring his wife they would at least try to keep the water without violence. But he knew it was too late. Stryker had seen to that.

Miranda served the water and Elizabeth took the opportunity to change the subject. She was beginning to worry about how this water thing would turn out and didn't want to pursue the matter. "Bill, Susan wants to see the sunset out at Hawk's Vista today."

Cavin and Elizabeth stared at each other until finally Cavin said, "Stryker, will you take her out there? Susan likes to watch the sun go down behind the Sierra's. She knows the way."

"Yes." Stryker wondered why the long looks Bill and Elizabeth gave each other seemed so serious.

"Better take the buckboard. I'll have it brought around," Cavin said.

"I need to wash up first. How long's the ride?" Stryker drained the water in the glass.

"About an hour each way, Susan can't take much more than that. It's painful for her. Might be her last trip out there." Cavin ignored Elizabeth who had suddenly jerked her head toward her husband.

"Full moon tonight," Cavin noted. "Shouldn't be too hard to see the trail on the way back. You'll have to go slow anyway, so's not to jostle Susan." He flung himself from the chair and made for the bar. "I need a drink, how about you, Stryker?"

"I'll wash up now." Stryker saluted a thank you with the water glass. "Figure 'bout an hour 'fore we leave."

"Yeah," Cavin confirmed.

"Thank you, Stryker," Elizabeth said, as he walked past her. "She'll be ready then."

As Stryker walked down the plastered hallway to his room, he heard Cavin say, "Liz, it's what she wants."

An hour later Stryker left his room, feeling fresh from using the wash basin to shave and wipe his body down with a wet cloth. He wore a clean shirt and denims Elizabeth had washed for him while he'd been riding with her husband. Susan sat in the wheelchair, waiting. Elizabeth and Susan offered Stryker small agreeable smiles, recognizing the mixed-breed's effort in making himself more presentable.

Cavin, nodded a greeting without a smile. "Let's go." He wheeled Susan to the front porch where the buckboard was waiting. Elizabeth followed. She bent to hug Susan, and Stryker noticed Mrs. Cavin's eyes were filled with tears when she straightened. Cavin lifted Susan from the chair and carried her down the steps. The ranch hand who'd brought the wagon up with a bed pillow on the seat, stood with one foot in the wagon box and the other braced against the toe board. Together, the men got the crippled girl onto the seat. She grimaced as she adjusted herself on the pillow.

Cavin put the wheelchair in the wagon and came up to Stryker. "Drive slow Stryker and try not to jolt her too much. He moved past Stryker and laid a big rough hand on one of Susan's. "We'll be here when you get back, honey." Susan returned a broken grin.

Stryker went around the wagon and eased himself onto the buckboard seat, being careful not to jostle Susan as he climbed on. A gentle snap on the reins and the four horses started out at a walk. Cavin joined his wife on the porch. He put his arm around her, and they waved goodbye even though they knew neither Susan nor Stryker saw them wave. "You know Liz, that man is one strange son-of-a-bitch. He'll kill a man who crosses him—won't bat an eye. But he won't steal from him, even if he's dead." Liz looked up at her husband who continued watching Stryker and Susan ride off.

They'd ridden about three miles when Susan asked, "You married Stryker?"

"No." *No small talk from the girl,* he thought.

"Ever been married?" Susan watched the dirt road ahead.

"Yes." *Why is she asking?*

"Me too. He left when I got hurt. She die?" Susan pressed her palms against the wagon seat and lifted her butt.

Stryker saw the movement from the corner of his eye and reined the horses even slower.

"Yes, been dead several years now."

"You still miss her?"

Stryker snapped his head to the girl, but she remained focused on the road. *Why are you asking me this?* He turned back to horses. "I miss her very much." *What the hell, this girl won't live much longer.*

"I miss my husband too; I loved him. Mostly my own fault he left. I was nasty to him, angry about what happened to me. Didn't think he could love a cripple, and he was only staying out of pity. Rather be alone than have his pity. How'd she die?"

"Artillery shell." *Shit!*

"An accident."

"Yes."

"Do you ever think you'll see her again?"

God Almighty! What the Hell? "Sometimes."

"I want to see Richard again, but not as a cripple. Was she pretty?"

"Yes."

"Tell me about her."

In all the years since Leigh died no one had ever asked him about her, not even Morgan. For a moment, Stryker thought about not answering, but the request brought back Leigh's face. "She had blond hair and blue eyes. Thin, but she always held herself straight, and she made me a better man." He paused. "That was when she lived. I'm not a good man now."

"I can tell you really miss her. What's her name?" Susan continued as in the present.

"Leigh."

"Stryker, I'll die before you, I'm sure. If I see Leigh, I'll tell her you miss her. Anything else?"

"How much farther to Hawk's Vista?"

"We're coming to a fork on the right. Take it. In a mile or so, we'll reach a bluff that overlooks a wide creek. That's it." Susan pressed her palms down again. "Joe's being a real asshole."

The forked road, less traveled than the main trail, was rougher and Stryker took another twenty minutes to reach the overlook. He eased off the buckboard and stepped behind to lift out the wheelchair. He rolled it up by the seat.

He scooped an arm under Susan's legs and carefully circled her torso with the other one. Lifting her off the buckboard seat as gently as he could, he positioned her above the chair. Susan wrapped her arms around his neck with her face close to his.

"Don't put me down yet," she whispered to him. "Kiss me."

Stryker leaned closer to Susan, looked into her eyes, and brought his mouth to her lips. Not passionate, he gave her a gentle, lingering kiss. And he tasted the salty liquid that flowed down her cheeks. When they parted he saw the tears in her eyes.

He set her in the chair and rolled her to the edge of the bluff. Below the water ran swift and clear. Beyond the creek, tall grass swaying in a soft breeze spread out to the foothills of the Sierras that rose majestically upward. Its shoulders hung coated in evergreens, and its head was crowned with white snow. The sun, a bright orange orb, drifted lower and seemed to melt into the snow.

"So beautiful, isn't it?" Susan breathlessly said.

"Yes, it is."

"Now Stryker, aren't you supposed to do something?"

It's called cohesion, the process which moves water from the ground and up a plant. It describes Stryker's realization of the real purpose for bringing Susan to Hawk's Vista. It seemed to rise from his boots to his brain. *Cavin's favor.*

"Please Stryker." Those were Susan's last words. The last thing she heard was a click of the Colt's hammer.

The .44 slug entered behind her left ear and blew a chunk of her brains out the right side of her head.

He stood on the bluff for a half hour, looking at the Sierras, thinking about the girl. Then he took her shawl and wound it tight around her head, which had stopped most of its massive draining. He laid her body in the buckboard and covered it with the blanket she'd worn over her legs. Stryker shoved the wheelchair off the bluff.

By the time he returned to the ranch it was dark. Bill and Elizabeth were waiting on the front porch along with two ranch hands. "Take the wagon 'round back" was all Cavin had to say. When Stryker pulled the buckboard behind the house, he saw three more ranch hands a way off with lit lanterns. "Over there, Stryker." Cavin said, pointing. He and Elizabeth, along with the two ranch hands continued walking toward the freshly dug grave.

The men placed the body in a wooden coffin and lowered it into the ground. Cavin offered a few words, and the men filled the grave with dirt. When the grave was filled, one by one the ranch hands filed by Stryker and shook his hand. None spoke.

"Bill couldn't do it," Elizabeth said to Stryker when they'd all gone in the house.

"None of us could," Cavin added. The other men shook their heads no as if apologizing.

"She begged us all," Elizabeth added. "And she started starving herself ten days ago."

Stryker gathered his belongings from the room and went out to the roan. He'd finished putting his things in the saddlebags when Elizabeth who'd been quietly standing on the porch, said "Thank you Stryker." He mounted and rode off in the night.

No one asked about the wheelchair.

CHAPTER NINE

Stryker rode north heading to Bishop Creek and eventually on to Laws, but he stopped to camp for the night after an hour's ride. He would have stayed at the Cavin Ranch and left in the morning except for the rationalizing and the lamentations. Neither of which he wanted to suffer through. He unsaddled the roan, tethered it to a rope line between two cottonwoods, and dropped a half sack of oats on the ground. After building a small fire, he boiled coffee and munched on leftover hardtack Elizabeth had put in his saddlebags for the ride south with Cavin. When finished eating and washing out the utensils, he lay on the saddle and looked up at the stars in the sky. *Shit*–Susan invoked memories of Leigh; of course, both dead at his hand. Gentle souls, lives cut short. One he'd abetted–or at least that's how he viewed killing Susan–one he'd betrayed, betrayed Leigh because his carelessness cut her life short. A failure he'd never forgive himself for. The two women might've been good friends. Stryker gazed at two distant stars twinkling close together, billions of miles from him–more than billions, more than miles. It took quite a long time before he finally fell asleep.

He woke with the canopy of stars glittering in the sky, daylight still an hour away. He threw off the saddle blanket and pulled on his boots. *Strange*, he thought, *no nightmares about Leigh*. It sure seemed as if it would have been the time to have one of the more shitty ones. No, last night he didn't dream at all. Rested, that's how he felt. *Couldn't be*, he thought morosely because he blew out a woman's brains. He was alone again. Maybe his own company agreed with him.

The stars had retreated, giving way to a dull gray by the time Stryker booted the stirrup and swung in the saddle. A half hour on the trail and streaks of sunlight lit the peaks of the snow-capped Sierras. He resisted the urge to stop and admire the view. He also fought against dwelling on how he'd confided about his dead wife to Susan. Shit, he'd blabbed on like a silly gossip. Well, Susan sure *ain't* gonna spread it around. The girl talked straight, without bullshit, as someone who is about to die does. Susan knew during that entire ride her life would end last night. Yes, he fought against thinking about that, but he lost the fight.

Stryker managed to wrench his thoughts away from the dead girl and shift to the water problem before he rode into Bishop Creek. It wouldn't take long for news of the aqueduct shooting and the work stoppage to reach town. He skirted the main part of Bishop Creek for now and ride west looking for the Gaines ranch. He remembered Cleo mentioning it was about six miles east of town. Tall grass reached up to scratch the belly of the roan as Stryker guided the big horse off the trail and angled northeast. Bishop Creek buildings came into view off to his left, but then they grew smaller as he rode eastward. Presently, he came to a wagon trail running east-west along the North fork of Bishop Creek, and he took it going east until the creek emptied into the Owens River. The land stretched flat in the broad valley with sparse clumps of trees rising from a sea of tall grass. Stryker spotted a modest single-story, adobe ranch house nesting under a stand of Aspen trees. It rested on a small rise maybe two-hundred feet north of where the creek joined a bend in the river. A herd of cattle grazed along the creek but nowhere near the size of the Cavin spread. Stryker pulled up the roan in front of the house.

Gunner came out on the stoop first, then Cleo, followed by Shane.

"Mister Stryker, c'mon inside." Gunner waived an arm, motioning toward the front door.

"Good to see you again." Cleo smiled and added. "We thought you left and wouldn't be back. You rode off without tellin'."

Stryker dismounted and looped the reins over the hitching rail. He wouldn't be long. The house foundation lay even with the ground, no front porch or deck of any kind, and Stryker followed the family through the door. What acted as a rug in the entryway was a trail of dried mud on the planked floor brought in with dirty boots. Inside, accommodations were sparse. Furniture consisted of straight-back chairs and a few small wooden tables, all but one of which held jars of paint, brushes, and half-finished paintings. All the sumptuous trappings sat in a ten by ten-foot room. Two closed doors probably led to bedrooms. A small alcove on the far side of the room had a wood-fired stove and a door leading outside. The only window in the place looked as if a hole had simply been punched out on the adobe wall to Stryker's left. The *window* did have shutters; two upright boards slid back and forth in a grooved slat beneath the opening, and inside another one on top, holding the vertical boards in place. One could open and close the window by moving the boards from side to side. Stryker could tell Baca was *real* handy with a hammer.

Cleo noticed Stryker passing judgement on the meager dwelling and offered a quick excuse, "We haven't been here long and there's still a lot to do." They'd lived in the house for three years, and the last nail driven in it was two summers ago. Gunner had no idea why his wife said that. He just stood there grinning.

"Would you like water or coffee?" Cleo asked.

"Coffee."

"Sit down. I'll pour you some." Cleo spun about and practically skipped across the room to the kitchen where a coffee pot rested on the stove.

The four of them, including Shane, took chairs around the only bare table. The boy also asked his mother for a cup of the brew. Stryker put up with small talk for a few minutes and then said, "Those men from Los Angeles are building a canal. They aim to take your water."

"I knew it!" Cleo exclaimed. Gunner snapped his head toward his wife with a surprised look on his face. "I knew they were up to no good," she continued, ignoring Gunner. "I tried to tell everyone. Nobody would listen. What can we do to stop 'em, Stryker?"

"The head of the aqueduct is about six miles south of Big Pine. I don't know how far it stretches back to Los Angeles," Stryker said. "Had a run in with three of 'em. Construction's halted for a while."

"Why'd they stop?" Gunner shifted his eyes from Cleo and interjected himself into the conversation. He tried to be relevant.

Cleo threw a dismissive shrug at Stryker acknowledging her husband's inadequacies. "I know it Stryker. It just happened. Don't ask me why. I don't know why. But a flower's gotta bloom where it's planted."

Stryker figured Cleo meant she put up with Gunner's faults to have a house and father for Shane. *Or maybe, Elfego has a wart on his pecker.*

"A gunfight?" Shane yelled excitedly.

"Quiet, Shane!" Cleo barked. "Will there be more trouble Stryker?"

"No. Not right now."

"They're giving up?"

"There'll be more men, more guards. Either you get the town to fight or you'll lose your water."

"These people are fools," Cleo huffed. "They refuse to believe Los Angeles that far away would take the water."

"Another rancher saw it." Stryker left out Cavin's name. No need to bring him up just yet. "Thanks for the coffee." Stryker pushed away from the table and got to his feet. He'd begun to walk across the planks and out of the house when he stopped and turned around. "Gonna be a fight." He spoke directly to Baca, ignoring Cleo. "I'll need your help. Be back in a day, maybe two."

Gunner rose and followed Stryker to the door and closed it. "He thinks he so smart, don't he?" Gunner groused as he sat at the table again. "What makes him so sure we'll have to fight?"

"We will," Cleo replied, resolutely.

"And what makes him so sure we won't have trouble with them men he ran into? Ain't they with the others?"

"They're dead dear."

Baca already figured as much. He also figured his impersonation of Gunner was nearing an end. Either he revealed himself as Elfego Baca soon and take his chances on still being able to service the two women, or leave and return as Gunner later. If there was gonna be trouble he,

Baca, couldn't stand around and watch. He'd grown tired of playing a dumb-assed artist anyway. He'd needed the disguise to conceal his identity as a gunfighter, but fucking the two women was getting complicated. It'd be a shame to survive all those men's bullets, only to get gunned down later by a jealous woman.

Outside, Stryker unhitched the roan and mounted. He swung the big horse around and headed for Laws. Killing the three men down south meant more men would come up from Los Angeles, and they wouldn't be civil engineers. He didn't give a shit about the water mess. Everyone could drink dirt as far as he was concerned. But Hearst had saved his life and paid him a hundred-thousand dollars for the first job, a ridiculous amount of money for collecting on a poker debt–the deed to the Examiner Newspaper. Stryker completed the job sure enough. He'd killed a few men, but he got it done. Could walk away, sure, but there is that damn woman, Morgan. *Shit. Something about her, and not just the way she fucked.* Her principals, what she stood for–truth. She stands for truth. It was she who really convinced him to come to Bishop Creek. Morgan told him Job Harriman, organizer of the Los Angeles Socialist Party, was behind the water grab, along with two other men, Werner the crafty commissioner and Books the brilliant engineer. The rally cry, "For the Common Good" trampled individual rights–water rights. Senator Hearst got wind of the plot to deceive the land owners in Owens Valley, the irrigation ruse. Morgan said George didn't fully understand the politics, but he knew of the underhandedness of it, and that was enough for him. Besides, Morgan wanted him to help, and she had always been on the right side. Stryker didn't want to let Hearst down, and he sure didn't want to let Morgan down. Strange how he, a vicious killer, now found himself owing allegiance to those two. Would he feel the same if he were on a mission to deceive, like those men from Los Angeles? To steal water? No, he reasoned. He'd been sucked in by Morgan mostly, to fight for her cause. But it was the right cause, and that wasn't a bad thing. Stryker never gave much thought to causes, although he fought for the North in the war. Making a man a slave didn't exactly sit well with him; however, as a boy in his teens, he didn't carry a banner for or against it. He got recruited and ended up in a blue uniform. Yeah, he was a mean son-of-a-bitch, he admitted, but he had his own code. Stryker sat straighter in the saddle.

He continued to skirt Bishop Creek, and about a mile on the other side of town he got back on the trail to Laws. The afternoon sun lengthened the cottonwood's shadows, and at first, Stryker didn't recognize the Conestoga wagon a half mile ahead. The wagon rested at an angle so that "Brother Elvin and the Righteous Sisters'" splayed on the canopy was out of view until Stryker rode by on the road. When he saw the lettering, he wheeled the roan and headed over toward the wagon.

Hany spotted Stryker first. "Elvin! Hey, you'all, Eula, Jemima, it's Mister Elvin!" But was that his real name? She wondered. "Is Elvin your real name, Elvin?" Hany asked after running up to him.

"Stryker." Elvin had been a mistake on his part in the first place. He would have given Elvin a bad name. The corner of his mouth twitched.

"Hey, you'all, it's Mister Stryker!" Hany yelled out, walking Stryker and the roan to the wagon.

Stryker stayed in the saddle when he got to the Conestoga. He rested his forearms on the saddle horn and watched Eula and Jemima pile out from back of the wagon.

"Stryker!" Jemima screamed his new name. She dashed across the short grass toward him and Stryker thought she would hug his leg hanging in the stirrup, but she pulled up short and out of breath. She stood next to the roan and petted its neck instead.

"Where you been Stryker?" Jemima asked, posing the question somewhere between resentment and a pout. "We been a sangin' at tha revival. An' the other Elvin, he's doing real good an' all, shakin' an' sangin', but we'all sure missed ya. You ain't come to the revival, have ya?" She said, caressing the roan's neck.

"Out here for a reason." Stryker asked as a statement, climbing off the roan.

"They won't let us camp near town, much less stay *in* town. So we keep outta people's way an' go in at preachin' time," Eula answered. "You seen Elvin? The other Elvin? He's been gone all day now. You know, Poenabe Truckee, that Paiute boy."

"We have another four days of revival," Hany chimed in. "We be gettin' ready to go in, in a little while. You see the tent Stryker?"

Stryker shook his head.

"It's big!" Jemima exclaimed. It's bigger we ever sung at! There must be 'hunerds of 'em!"

"We need Elvin, less'n you wanna do it, Stryker." Eula said.

"Be watching for him on the way to Laws. See which way he headed." Stryker *asked*.

"No. But he do a lotta talkin' last night, Stryker."

"Tell me." Stryker said.

Eula explained further, "After we done our sangin' he went on about how the whites–ain't meanin' you, Stryker–stole them injun's water, an' how them other whites down south gonna steal it even more."

"What happened then?" Stryker actually asked a question as a question.

"Nothin', they's a lotta grumblin' an' such, but weren't nobody causin' a ruckus, I reckon." Eula cast a quick glance at Hany and Jemima. "Y'all got anythin' more?"

Hany spoke up. "Last we see'd him he was goin' off with that Paya girl. That was last night right after the preachin'."

"Ain't see'd him since," Jemima volunteered. "An' he come by for to practice ever day, way 'fore now. Don't wanna say they's sinful, but I think them's a lot women come to tha preachin' just to see Elvin," Jemima giggled.

"People talking about water canal coming to Bishop Creek," Stryker said.

"They is?" Eula acted surprised at the news, then she realized when Stryker didn't elaborate, he was asking her about it. "No, we ain't heared nothin'."

Stryker stepped to the roan, threw a boot in the stirrup, and heaved himself onto the roan's back. "I'll watch for Elvin." He wheeled the roan north and spurred its flanks. News of the canal killings would have surely reached Bishop Creek by now, Stryker speculated. The telegraph made news travel faster these days. It occurred to him though, the Los Angeles bunch might have wanted to keep the killings quiet for now.

Spreading the news about the shootings would also reveal an aqueduct snaking up the valley.

The day aged to the middle of a hot and muggy afternoon. Even at four-thousand feet altitude, the sun can be oppressive. Stryker guided the roan to where a creek widened to a ten-foot pool, seemingly resting there in the tall grassy meadow before continuing its journey south. He dismounted and led the horse to the water. He let it drink while he filled his canteen a few feet upstream. Lifting the canteen to his mouth, he surveyed the landscape as he drank. Snow crowning the peaks of the Sierra's hung high in the sky as a sharp contrast to the sweltering heat in the valley below. A hundred yards upstream a cluster of cottonwoods, willows, and aspen trees huddled around the creek offering shade. Stryker took the reins, wrestled the roan's muzzle from the water, and led the roan toward the inviting shade. Limber tree branches on the willow trees billowed out and down with their tips tickling the ground. Stryker pushed through them to reach an open grassy area within. He pulled the saddle and blanket from the roan, leaving on the headstall. Using twenty feet of rope he tied the horse to a cottonwood sapling, allowing it to graze in lush grass by the creek. He withdrew a cut of hardtack and a biscuit from his saddlebag and sat on the saddle to eat while he watched the roan graze. When finished, he took a swig of water from the canteen and let his eyes take in more of his surroundings.

That's when Stryker discovered he wasn't alone. On the far side of the clearing, perhaps a hundred paces or so, and among more cottonwoods and willows, he glimpsed something. Mostly hidden by trees, it looked suspicious. It had a pale color, neither green nor brown, but a light tan, and its shape was strangely vertical, hung above the ground. He pulled the Winchester. Moving stealthily among the trees, Stryker worked his way around the clearing. Carefully moving among the willow branches, he kept the cottonwood trunks between him and what he guessed to be a field-dressed animal. Warily halting and kneeling every few feet, he peered at what he could see through the trees and listened. Dead silence. Finally, he got to where only one large cottonwood separated him from what he'd spotted from the other side of the clearing. He took off his hat and laid it on the ground. Raising the carbine to his shoulder, he moved up against the tree trunk. He carefully peeked around the right side. The carbine barrel led the way.

The naked bodies of Poenabe and Paya hung facing one another. Hands tied behind them, their feet were only a few inches above the ground, but high enough. Flies crawled in and out of their eyes, noses, and mouths laying eggs. Some of which had already hatched into maggots. Stryker figured that meant the young Paiutes were hanged the night before. Elvin and Paya danced their last dance at end of a rope. It didn't take a lot of reasoning to know who arranged the dances. Although Stryker couldn't know for sure if Poenabe's revival speech triggered the hanging, it likely played a part in it. And, he now realized, the bunch from Los Angeles wasn't scared off by the canal shootings. No doubt Texas, the man he killed in the stable, worked for Ralston, and the other men at Stella's Boarding House did too. Ralston, the councilman, and Werner and Book, the Los Angeles men Cleo talked about, probably know each other. How many more guns were in Bishop Creek, or on their way, Stryker could only guess. There's a lot more cockroaches in the kitchen than the ones you see on the floor.

Stryker stayed behind the cottonwood and did a quick scan with the carbine before returning to the roan. He went back the same route he'd taken through the trees, only quicker this time. The roan nickered a greeting. Stryker led the horse across the creek, still carrying the 44-40, and mounted up after leaving the cottonwoods. He thought about sending a telegram to Hearst but changed his mind. *That damn Baca better put down his fucking paintbrush and pick up a gun.*

Stryker rode to Libra's house coming in from the north, having skirted west of Laws to avoid riding through town. Not knowing what help he could count on in Bishop Creek meant recruiting in Laws, and the only person he knew there was Libra. Another reason to not kill Orlo, Libra could've gotten that big black lover to help.

Dusk settled in, and he saw a light in the back of the house. He tied the roan by the cottonwood behind the house and entered Libra's back door.

"Stryker!" Libra exclaimed. She was shucking corn cobs.

Stryker couldn't tell if she were actually surprised, or glad to see him.

She had her hair coiled on top of her head, and wore a white shirt with rolled-up sleeves over a mid-calf skirt, and was barefooted. Her revealed neck looked slender and elegant. High cheekbones added to her surprising attractiveness. *What a waste.*

"What are you doing here?" She ignored Stryker's failure to knock.

"Cleo tell you about the water."

"Some." Libra put down a corncob.

Stryker played the environmentalist card. "There's a bad bunch up from Los Angeles here to take the water. That'll leave the Indians and the wildlife in the valley without water." He left out the ranchers, assuming Libra's bleeding heart didn't extend to them.

"Oh, my goodness! Cleo never told me that!" Libra cocked her head sideways. "Mister Stryker, you don't look like a man who'd be caring about those kind of causes."

"We need all the help we–you can get, to stop them. Cleo told me about how you feel about guns. We'll have to use 'em to save the water for animals and savages."

"They're not savages. They're Native Americans, as ones with nature–earth, wind, and water." Libra waved her hand upward and outward, palm ending skyward. "Water–they want to take the water?" She dropped her arms. "Oh, we must stop that!"

"Yes, that's right. Who'll fight this terrible destruction of nature?" Stryker's stomach turned. He decided not to inform Libra about Poenabe and Paya. No need for the heavy guns, and he didn't want to be tied to the hanging. No doubt the woman would blab to everybody he'd discovered the bodies. Questions should be directed at others, not him.

"You know men in Laws to help, Libra?" Stryker asked again. He now regretted coming to see the nature woman. "Men who know how to use a gun," Stryker stressed. *Yes, a fucking gun dammit.*

"Stryker, I hear boots on the front porch!" Libra's surprise sounded genuine. "Maybe you better wait in the kitchen." Libra pivoted quickly. The skirt billowed and swirled trying to catch up, and she ran down the hall. Someone rapped at the door. She crossed the front room and gripped the doorknob, but didn't turn it. "Who there?"

Stryker waited for Libra to reach the living room and followed, the

Peacemaker drawn and cocked. He remained in the hallway, flattened against a wall.

"It's me, Miss Libra—Jonas. I got Milford with me. Can we come in and talk?"

Libra opened the door four inches. "Hello, Jonas." She dipped her head at the man behind him. "Mister Milford. What's this about?" She'd seen the two before, even spoke to them a few times when she visited the hardware store, but knew little about them. They'd always seemed friendly, though.

"Nothing with you ma'am," Jonas was quick to say. "We was hoping you could tell us where we might find that feller who come by the other day, the one who killed the Negro."

"If I see him again, I'll tell him." Libra pushed on the door to close it.

"Wait." Jonas pushed back. "We . . . Miss Libra, can we just come in for a minute?"

"All right, come in." Libra ushered in the men with a loud voice, trusting that Stryker would hear her and leave. "Sit down, gentlemen." Libra sat quickly in her favorite chair, an old covered wingback. She wanted the conversation in the front room.

Stryker stepped back and slipped inside the downstairs bedroom. He eased the door closed, leaving it cracked open to listen. Enough waning daylight drifted through the window, allowing Stryker to see the only pieces of furniture in the room were a brass bed, a nightstand, and a wooden chair. Libra could've told the men he was there, or maybe had been there, but she didn't. So far, the men weren't posing an immediate threat. Besides, he wanted to hear what they had to say about the killings and the canal. He kept his ear by the opening.

The two men took seats opposite Libra, Milford on the settee, and Jonas on a straight-back chair. Both men appeared to be in their sixties, portly, dressed in dusty black suits, and unarmed. Milford nervously rotated the derby hat between his knees, waiting for Jonas to start. Jonas placed his hat on a table.

"There's been a killing south of Bishop Creek. Two men ambushed a work crew and kilt three of the workers. They say one of them men who done the killing looked a lot like that man I was talking about, you know, the one who come by here." Jonas looked to Milford for confirmation. Milford nodded. "'Cept for the negro, we ain't had a killing 'round here for a long while. Most of us don't carry guns as you can see, Miss Libra. Now we've had four in just a few days."

"I've already told you, if I see him, I'll tell him you're looking for 'im," Libra said curtly. "Why'd he shoot them? He did shoot 'em, I suppose."

"Yes ma'am, they wuz surely shot." Jonas answered. "The story goes they's—the men working down there, that is—wuz digging some kind of a big ditch. Tha two men rode up an' saw tha diggin', an' they all got to arguing. Then the shootin' started, an' three of them doin' the diggin' got kilt."

"Who was the other man? You said two." Libra asked.

"Not sure, he could be just about anybody. Big man, so we reckon that descript-shun' would fit a lot fellers. No mistakin' the man wit' him tho'. He kinda stands out, real mean lookin' an' all."

"That's true enough," Libra agreed. "What was the digging—you said something about a ditch—what was that for? Do you know?"

"No ma'am, we ain't sure 'bout that part."

"Well, is there anything else?" Libra rose from her chair.

"No, I reckon not." Jonas got to his feet. Milford did as well. "Just send word if you will, that is, if you come across 'im again." Jonas turned toward the door but swung back. He offered a nervous smile and said, "Thank you, Miss Libra. You've been right kind with your time." Jonas continued out the house. Milford trailed behind.

Libra spun around and started down the hall. She made it halfway before meeting Stryker coming out from the bedroom. She placed a hand on his chest and pushed him back. "No, wait. They might still be looking around. Is your horse out there?" Without waiting for Stryker's answer, Libra said, "You best stay in the house for a while."

Stryker allowed Libra's entreaties, still curious why she hadn't told Jonas about him. He stepped away from the door.

"I don't want you men shooting up my house," Libra said. She failed to point out Jonas and Milford were unarmed—although Stryker already knew it. "You men are all alike. You start shootin' at each other 'fore anything else. What is it with you?" She wagged her fore-finger at Stryker. "Did you shoot those three men Jonas was talking about?"

Stryker strolled to the bed. He took off the Stetson and sailed it cn the coverings. He flopped on the bed, clasped his hands behind his head, and crossed his ankles. The boots hung off the end of the bed. With an iced stare of the steel-gray eyes, he told her yes.

Libra assumed he had, however the casualness of his reply shocked her. "Why?"

"They needed to stop living."

Libra bit her lip. "Were they shooting at you first? I mean, threatening in any way?" She hesitated a moment and then asked, "Did they have guns they were gonna shoot, at least? For God's sake say yes."

"One had a shotgun."

"The other two?"

"They were with the man with a shotgun."

Libra seemed to relax a little, accepting Stryker's answer, giving him a smidgen of benefit. She scooted the chair close to the bed and sat. "Did they die right away?"

That's an odd question, woman. "'Bout as long as it takes to die from acute lead poisoning," Stryker said.

"Did they say anything when they was dying?" Libra nervously breathed the question, her fingers playing with the top shirt button.

"Don't recall," Stryker said, watching her fingers fumble with the button. He wondered if, incredibly, the woman was getting excited.

"Their eyes, was their eyes open? They look at you? Did you watch 'em back?" Libra's lower lip trembled.

"Made sure the fellow with the shotgun was dead." Now Stryker was *really* curious. Libra's eyes gleamed with excitement. She unbuttoned the top button and fingered the two small bones at the base of her throat.

"Could you tell the exact moment he died?" Her voice trembled.

"You getting bothered woman?"

"Yes!" She blew out the yes with a pent-up blast of air. She grabbed his arm and placed his hand on her chest. "Feel my heart!" Libra held Stryker's hand tight against her and worked another button loose.

"Here." She shoved his hand inside the shirt, next to her left breast. "Feel how fast!"

"No Libra, not . . ."

"No, we won't." She twisted her torso, positioning her breast under Stryker's hand. "Just feel it, that's all." She held his hand on her breast, and moved her free hand lower, much lower. She lifted the hem of her skirt. No undergarments, but Stryker missed that. The skirt fell when she released it. She spread her knees and her fingers flew to a very wet quim. "Ohhh . . ." Libra groaned in rapture as she threw back her head. She withdrew her dripping fingers, and using the tips of the middle three, began making circular motions on an engorged clitoris. Libra righted herself, and looking at Stryker in the fading light said, "Feel my breast. I'll do the rest."

She moved his hand around her breast. A little droopy but not over-sized. *Not bad Libra.*

"Please, move your fingers." Libra pressed on his fingers. "Squeeze my nipple."

Stryker did as she asked. Libra was under obvious duress.

"Yes, that's it." The hand below moved faster. "Pull on it! Pinch it. Pull hard! That's it–hard!"

Minutes passed. Libra rested. Maybe she was teasing herself. She started up again, urgently. Lost in pleasure. Except for Stryker's hand, she ignored him. Without warning, her body stiffened. Her hand stopped moving. "Ahhhhh . . ." She closed her mouth. A groan that began in her toes, crawled up her body, and ended in a loud grunt. In a few seconds, her hand got busy again, and she had another orgasm.

Libra rested few minutes, catching her breath. Then she said, "Feel my other breast."

Libra guided Stryker's hand to her right breast. He did his part. She started slow and worked herself to more orgasms. None quite as good as the first one though, and Libra stopped after number five. She lifted Stryker's hand from her breast and kissed it. Keeping the back of his hand pressed against her face, she shut her eyes, and caressed the leathery skin with her cheek.

"Are you hungry?" Libra asked, coming out of her trance. She quickly straightened her skirt and re-buttoned the buttons as if suddenly embarrassed.

No problem on this end, Libra. "No."

"A drink then; I don't have anything stronger than coffee."

"That'll do."

Libra rose to her feet, swept her hands down her skirt, and abruptly left the bedroom for the kitchen.

Stryker lifted his legs off the bed, readying to swing them to the floor, and realized he had a stiffening in his loins. Apparently, he mused, he'd been so busy watching Miss Nature please herself he wasn't aware of his own arousal. Shame. He got off the bed and went to the kitchen where Libra could not help but notice the big bulge in his pants. She poured the coffee without comment.

"Mister Stryker, those men who come here, they're looking for you."

"I heard. Didn't catch all of it." He accepted a cup of warm coffee and caught a whiff of Libra's ardor on her fingers. Libra saw him eyeing her hand and hurriedly dropped it, hiding the offending appendage in a fold of her skirt.

"They said you found some men digging a ditch." Libra pounced on a less personal subject. "And that's when you shot 'em."

"Digging a canal, an aqueduct, for the water here."

"All the way to Los Angeles?" Libra dropped into a chair across from Stryker. "How much of the water, you think?"

"All of it."

CHAPTER TEN

"Killed three of 'em, you say?" Fred Werner asked, a worried scowl on his handsome face.

"Maybe four," Ralston added. "I think Texas had a run-in wit' somebody in that stable. They said he had a stroke. I ain't so damn sure." The councilman glared at Werner and then at Books. Five men sat in an upstairs room. Councilmen brothers, Peter and Sandy, waddled up the stairs of the Bishop Creek Hotel to join Commissioner Werner, Books, his engineer, and the other Bishop Creek councilman, Ralston.

"Any idea who's behind the killings?" Werner asked. "How many? I mean, is there one or two ranchers or we fightin' against the whole valley here?"

Peter and Sandy looked at Ralston to answer. "Well, there was two down at the diggin'. Some of tha men down there said one was a tall, mean-looking son-o-bitch, an' the other'n was a big man too. That's all we know. 'Cept the mean bastard mighta been the fella I met at Stella's. He looked like the kind of son o' bitch who'd do killin' like they done."

"Where's that man now, Eddie?" The commissioner used the more friendly name, rather than *Edward* because he needed his help. "You got somebody who'd find him and that other one too? Offer 'em money. Get 'em workin' for us instead. Ain't no reason they can't work for us. We might need someone like them fellas, if things get outta hand up here."

"I got Ashe an' R.J.," Ralston offered. "Ashe is pretty tough, but I ain't so sure he could handle that Stryker man if things turn ugly. See'd rattlers wit' better dispositshuns'. Cold, ghost-like gray eyes, and the way he wears his gun . . . got a feelin' he knows how to use it."

"Well, find him and talk to him anyway," Werner said. He leaned forward and rested his elbows on the table. His face took on an even more serious countenance. "Look here now. Los Angeles needs this water. An' we're gonna get it. I don't care what we gotta do. Ralston, you and your two fat friends here are being well paid, and I expect you to hold up your end of the bargain. If I have to, I'll expose you three in the paper back home and have it delivered up here. Folks in Bishop Creek might not like how you sold 'em out. They might even hang you." Werner allowed himself a crooked grin when the three councilmen suddenly sat up. That got their attention. They appeared uncomfortable. "I'll help you, though. It's time to bring up some of boys from down south. Men trained in procuring land rights." The commissioner smiled again.

"How many?" Ralston asked, still shaken, wondering if the men came with ropes. Councilmen, Peter and Sandy became more attentive as well.

"Oh, I don't know, twenty, twenty-five." Werner turned to Books. "What do you think, Cory?"

The chief engineer cleared his throat and said, "Yes, they should be sufficient."

"It'll take a few days for my boys to get up here. In the meantime, . . . oh, I almost forgot. Other night at church, I hear there was an Indian kid, dressed up in some kind of fancy outfit, spoutin' off about water rights for the Paiutes." Werner cleared his throat. "God damn, we gotta deal with the fuckin' Indians now too?"

"Ashe said he talked wit' 'im," Ralston said, perking up. "Said he an' R.J. persuaded the boy to back off," the councilman crowed. He flashed a nervous smile. It fled quickly.

"Well now Eddie, that's how to earn your pay," Werner said,

acknowledging Ralston's initiative with a sharp head dip. "Good, so that's the end of it? Won't givin' us more trouble then?"

"That's what Ashe told me." Ralston's confidence grew, "Said made sure won't have to worry none wit' em' causin' trouble. Don't know what he meant." Ralston shrugged his shoulders. "He don't care for the redskins. Probably beat 'im some I reckon."

"Until the boys get here, keep telling the landowners the state is putting in an irrigation system for 'em, and they have to sign over their water rights so we can do it. Don't say Los Angeles, tell 'em the state of California's doing it." Werner pointed his forefinger in the shape of a pistol at Books. "Cole, get a few of your men from the aqueduct and bring 'em up here. Show a survey crew working, lay out stakes an' string. Have 'em dig a fucking ditch or two. Might as well start laying out canals to feed into the main aqueduct, right?"

"Will do Fred." Books pulled a pencil and paper from his shirt pocket and scribbled down the instructions. Not that he needed to write a note for himself, he just wanted the commissioner to see him do it. "What about the digging down south, Fred? We start up again or wait for your men?"

"For the time being, Cole, pull the crews off the north end. Move down, I don't know . . . how far down would you say, ten miles or so? Far enough away where they think we've abandoned the job up here. You gotta dig it out there anyway. Just dig down there for a while. When my men show up, we'll dig where we damn well please."

"What about us, Fred?" Ralston asked. "What should we be doin'?"

"All right Eddie, you fellas up here keep talkin' 'bout the irrigation system we're gonna build here for them. Have a town meeting or something." Werner came around to being cordial to the councilmen again.

"Yeah, a town meeting," Ralston agreed. "I'll call a meeting. Make an announcement about how the state has to have the water rights, otherwise they'll still have to keep bringing their livestock—the cattle ranchers, I mean—to the river. Some have to go several miles you know." It almost sounded as if the councilman was actually making a good case for the irrigation system, the system which would never be built.

If Commissioner Frederick Werner recognized the rational for the irrigation network, he failed to show it. He responded to Ralston's comments with a good-natured wink and a warm smile. "That's right Eddie." Werner turned to his chief engineer again. "Cole, make sure what you do up here works for us. We can't afford to waste time, got to get that water flowing south as soon as we can." Nodding to Ralston and the two fat councilman brothers, Peter and Sandy, Werner said, "You boys can leave. I need to go over a few things with Cole."

"Fred? What is it?" Books looked puzzled. A private talk? He had no idea what it could be about.

"Cole, you're a civil engineer, not used to violence," Werner began. "But we're likely to have it, and I need to know you'll be with me no matter how rough it gets. They've already murdered three of your men, and that means these folks aren't gonna give up their water without a fight, a bloody one. But let me tell you, if we bring this water to Los Angeles, it won't be just me to be honored. I'll make sure you'll be the biggest hero that town has ever had. Streets, buildings, parks, schools—shit, I'll rename the God-damned town after you, we get the fuckin' water."

"Fred, I want to stand there by the aqueduct." Books said. "I wanna see the looks on their faces when I open the sluice gate and tell 'em, 'Here's the water, take it.' The town can keep its name, but I do wanna get rich."

"We'll both make a lot of money, Cole. I've put together a real estate syndicate and we've bought up property rights in the San Fernando Valley. The water's gonna flow right through it. A loan's already to be floated to buy the land from the syndicate and the taxpayers will pay back the loan. You build this aqueduct for me, and you'll be in the syndicate as one of the owners. I'll see to it."

"You'll get it, Fred, come hell or high water!" Books avowed.

Both men exploded in loud guffaws.

⚔

"No, ain't heared from him," Senator Hearst replied to Morgan's asking about Stryker. "No news neither on what's happenin' where he's at. No, that ain't right." Hearst paused, then continued, "Heared three men got shot somewhere south of Bishop Creek. An' now that I think of it, that does kinda sound like somethin' . . ." Hearst pensively turned the whiskey glass on the linen-covered table, studying it as if the liquid within contained hidden knowledge. He raised it and took a sip of knowledge. Returning the glass to the table, Hearst said, "I reckon we'll hear somethin' in due course."

Senator Hearst and Morgan Bickford sat at their usual discreet table in the corner table of Men's Grill Room at the Palace Hotel. Morgan wore her customary slacks, open-collared shirt with a leather jacket, and her haired pulled back in a tight ponytail. She could have passed as an effeminate male; the Grill Room was supposed to be for men only. The women having their own Ladies Grill, but it didn't matter. Senator Hearst commanded special privileges. They came with the luxury suite on the Palace's top floor and his political status. Allowing Hearst to dine with Morgan was one small way in which the hotel honored its special guests. The Palace had very strict rules, so that they could break them and thereby bestow these special privileges to favored guests like a United States Senator.

"Still, I'd like to hear how he's progressing."

The Senator offered a wry smile. He knew what Morgan really meant. She really wanted to know if her favorite killer was still alive. "I'll see what I can find out."

"George," only two people could call the Senator by his first name, his wife and the woman he wished was his wife, "What is your position on the water? Los Angeles must be a concern for you as well." Morgan seldom spoke idly. Her words were straight-arrow missives.

"That's true." Hearst readied himself for a conversation which he figured would make him squirm.

"You sent Stryker to help the ranchers."

"Yeah, yeah I did. Don't seem right to steal their water, but . . . ah hell, Morgan, I ain't so sure. They need it."

"George, 'need' is not a good reason to take what doesn't belong to them. People will always have needs. The robber needs a bank's money. The mugger needs a stranger's money. A man needs food for his family.

Does that give them all the right to steal it? You need votes. Would you steal them? Don't say yes. Los Angeles needs water. Bishop Creek needs the water. The difference is Bishop Creek owns it."

"Maybe the folks in Bishop would sell some of it. Wouldn't that be all right?" Hearst asked.

"Yes, if at a fair price to both," Morgan replied.

"Then, that's what they should do. If I have to get directly involved, that's what I'll have them do." Hearst reached across the table and patted the back of Morgan's hand.

"But, you shouldn't force either side, George." Morgan turned her hand over and gripped his as she made her point. "This is about big government. It's politicians, especially the Socialists among them, who are using their positions of power to strip from those ranchers and farmers what is rightfully theirs. There won't be any fair exchange."

Hearst was quite content to continue letting Morgan state her case as long as she held his hand. "Tell me more."

Morgan smiled and said, "I'm grateful for your help." She gave the Senator's hand a final squeeze and pulled hers back to lift her wine glass.

Hearst smiled at the attractive woman, raised his whiskey glass in a salute to her, and said, "I'll do what I can."

CHAPTER ELEVEN

Stryker left Libra's house reflecting on the woman and her visitors. The two men who came asking for him, unarmed and yet wanting to find him, posed a puzzle the mixed-breed couldn't quite figure out. He mounted the roan and turned south. *It's time Cleo knew who Gunner really was. He should have told her when he last saw them. Up to Cleo how she would explain Elfego to Shane. If Owens Valley keeps its water, they'll have to fight for it, and Baca is too good a gun for him to sit this out.*

Then, there's Libra. *He could have forced himself on her, probably not unwelcomed. The woman wasn't half bad looking either. Damn, she sure wanted it. Raw desire in a woman can sure arouse a man. Libra's wanting definitely had the little soldier at attention. Why hadn't he just taken her? Rape, he'd never done it. The only woman he ever came close to raping was the woman in San Francisco, Morgan–Morgan Bickford. And then after she stripped in front of him and asked–no demanded–he fuck her. Your honor, Morgan said to me 'fuck me if you're man enough'. Did you say that to mister Stryker, ma'am? The judge would ask. Yes. Case closed. Not that he would ever testify against her. He'd go to prison before that happened.* But that damn woman lit a fire in him other women can't do. *She's good-looking–yes, she moves well under him–*

yes–very yes. Her rigid principles; yes, that's the difference, that's what kindles the fire. Yeah, that about her makes *him* rigid. The corner of his lip twitched. Stryker then realized he hadn't forced himself on other women, Libra included, because he really didn't give a shit about them.

Stryker rode the roan inside the draw which angled southwest and away from Libra's house for roughly a hundred yards, remaining partially hidden out of view from watchful townspeople in Laws. The moon remained crouched behind a peak, slowly creeping up, and had yet to provide any light in the valley. Stryker pulled the reins right to guide the big horse up the gentle slope and out of the draw. He could see the outline of the large cottonwood standing guard where the north-south trail intersected with one running east-west. He did not see the two men waiting on the far side of the tree.

Stryker caught sight of movement near the cottonwood. He ducked down the roan's right side, drawing and cocking the Peacemaker. Fisting the roan's mane in his left hand, he hung under its neck.

"Hey thar, mister Stryker." A somewhat familiar voice called out. "We ain't armed. We'd like to talk with ya, if'n it's all right."

Jonas, Stryker recognized the caller as one of Libra's visitors. He eased his left leg off the saddle and dropped to the ground. He leaned over the saddle, keeping the horse between him and Jonas. The Colt remained cocked and pointed at the closest shadow by the cottonwood. He eased the carbine out of the scabbard with his free hand. If he had to fire the pistol he planned to leap into the draw for cover. The damn horse would probably bolt from the gunshot.

"Mister Stryker," Jonas called out again. "Don't shoot. We mean no harm."

"Come away from the tree where I can see you," Stryker ordered.

Jonas and Milford stepped cautiously away from the cottonwood, holding their hands aloft. "Like I told ya, we ain't armed," Jonas said a third time, trying to keep an eye on Stryker a hundred feet away. He tripped over a rock half-buried and fell on his face. "Don't shoot! I fell!" Jonas screamed with a mouthful of dirt. "Ah, damn it!" He cursed, slavering mud from his mouth.

Stryker heard Jonas's spitting and held fire.

Milford interceded, "We know you shot them diggers and . . . uh . . ."

"We just want to thank you, mister," Jonas said, rising to his feet, brushing road dust off his chest.

Milford added an awkward sounding thank-you as well.

"An' we wanna . . . well, we wanna offer you a job, sir," Jonas said, obviously struggling with the right words. The two men, encouraged by the lack of flying bullets, walked toward Stryker again. They got to within five feet of him and halted. Their encouragement grew even more when they heard the Peacemaker click as Stryker eased its hammer forward.

"Job." Stryker repeated. Jonas and his buddy probably couldn't tell if Stryker was asking or stating.

"Uh, a job, yes," Jonas said. "I'm Jonas. This is my partner here, Milford." Jonas dipped his head sideways at the other man. "We own the Laws Bank and Trust Company here."

"We also own the Laws Mercantile and Dry Goods Store, The Laws Sentinel, and the telegraph," Milford added. The full moon now provided enough light for Stryker to note a look of annoyance on Jonas's face.

"That's true. We took those over when they failed," Jonas supplied, sounding apologetic.

"We moved the telegraph office into the Laws Mercantile and Dry Goods Store," Milford added.

"Mister Stryker don't care about that, Milford," Jonas said. "We've got news . . ."

"I do care," Stryker interrupted. "What news."

Jonas continued, trying not to be flustered because of the interruptions. "In Los Angeles, my cousin . . ."

"Willard's your uncle, Jonas," Milford corrected.

"Lester's my cousin, damn it! He sent the telegram for Christ's sake! Willard, my uncle, heard from the commissioner's secretary–I think he knows that woman pretty good–and . . ."

"He's fuckin' her," Milford said.

"God Almighty! Will you just shut the hell up?" Jonas wailed.

"Anyway. . ." Jonas paused to make sure his partner was finished with his contributions. "About a month ago we got word they was gonna come up here and take our water. We tried to tell folks here and in Bishop Creek, but they all didn't believe us, 'cept Cleo, that is. She took it serious. Said she was writin' the governor. Don't know if she did or if he got it. We never heared nothing til the news two fellas shot three canal workers south of Bishop. One of the two was said to be you."

Stryker re-booted the .44-40 and walked around the roan. He lifted a boot to the stirrup.

"Wait! Don't you wanna hear 'bout the job?" Jonas asked hurriedly.

Stryker climbed into the saddle. "Already got one."

"We need our water protected here in Laws!" Jonas pleaded. "We can pay what you ask, mister Stryker." Jonas stepped forward, reached out to grab the reins, but thought that would be a bad idea. Stryker held the roan back.

"Those businesses of yours drink a lot of water," Stryker drawled.

"No, they don't," Jonas said. "But our customers, the ranchers and farmers, need the water. They don't have it; they go outta business, an' we will too."

"You'll need more than one gunman. Round up more men—ones who can use a gun. I'll meet you at Libra's. And Jonas, get your uncle to hump the secretary. Find out how many men they're sending." Stryker wheeled the roan, but before he spurred its flanks he warned, "I'll work with you, not for you. That means in two days when I return, you'll have shotguns and handguns loaded, and ready.

Jonas stepped back and asked, "By us? We ain't much good with firearms." Milford nodded in agreement, then quickly shook his head no.

"Get the guns and men to use 'em. Another thing, four nights from now, round up every wagon, buggy, and horse you can get, and have 'em at Libra's right after dark. Leave 'em there with an open space in front of the door." Spread word you're gonna have a meeting about the water. I'll see you then."

Stryker heeled his spurs on the roan.

"You think he's serious?" Milford asked.

"He's killed three men," Jonas said, watching Stryker ride out of sight.

Stryker veered from the trail to Bishop Creek and angled toward the Righteous Sister's wagon. They needed to know about Poenabe and Paya. *Should have told them earlier.* The moon, almost full, put out enough light for Stryker to pick his way across open ground in a direct route to their wagon. He saw the campfire's dying reflection on their prairie schooner. All three "righteous" sisters had climbed in the wagon for the night. They remained sequestered inside even after Stryker rode into camp. He brought the roan between the fire and the wagon where the women could surely see the imposing silhouette of horse and rider. Stryker, ever tactful, directed the announcement at the 'Elvin and The Righteous Sisters' painted on the side canvas, "Poenabe and Paya are dead."

The wailing began. Not just ordinary bawling, no, the Righteous Sisters, staying in the wagon, commenced such an ear-splitting lamentation, the coyotes as far away as Virginia City joined in.

Stryker, rightly figuring he had all he could stand in the first three seconds, rode off in the dark. The wailers realized he'd left a half hour later.

He made camp a couple miles east of Bishop Creek near the Owens River. Ordinarily, he found making camp in the dark a pain in the ass, but the brightness of the moon made the chore less challenging. He ate a few pieces of hardtack on a biscuit, washed down with water, and lay on the bedroll with the saddle for a pillow. While idly watching the star-lit sky, he contemplated the next move, a plan of action. Killing the men at the canal probably didn't help trying a less violent solution, but the man with a shotgun left little choice. The other two though? Stryker usually tied off loose ends; his enemies occupied graves. Well, not all, some were just left on the ground and scavengers ate 'em. Werner would no doubt bring up re-enforcements. There was gonna be a fight. All right, now he had to devise a plan where most if not all of those men died.

From the day young Stryker had watched his parents butchered in front of him, and subsequently made his first kill as a teenager, he was shaped, molded, and driven by violence and tragedy. He'd been calibrated to kill. Unfortunately for his adversaries, negotiations or peaceful mediations weren't in him. He found that quick and efficient deaths solved things the best. And for him, a fair fight happened by chance. He'd shoot an unarmed man in the back, if that man crossed him—problem solved, results final. His only judgement, indeed his only measure of success or failure–he lived, they died. Like a perpetually wounded animal, snarling, fangs always bared, he attacked anyone who came near. Stryker had no friends. He *never* had friends. There had been a brief respite with affection when married to Leigh. That would not happen again. He wouldn't allow it. Even the man, George Hearst, who had saved his life, paid him an enormous sum of money, could not be called friend. Hearst had his respect. That's all. Morgan, with her principles, her philosophy, had his admiration. Unlike the haunting dreams of Leigh, nightmares really, Morgan represented a temptress. She embodied everything a man like him could want, attractive, a damn good fuck, and brains. But for the jinx, he might be tempted to settle down with her. He'd played a part in Leigh's death though; he couldn't play a part in Morgan's too. *She sure is one hell of a woman.* He had no way of knowing of course; some decades later a woman-like Morgan would escape from a totalitarian state and write books affecting millions; her subject matter–objectivism, capitalism, and reason. Stryker held no such lofty ideals. His was simple pragmatism, the ultimate practical man. And now, he had to develop a practical plan to kill as many men from Los Angeles as he could.

Morning arrived with ground hugging fog. Stryker built a fire and boiled water to make coffee. He'd spent the night wrestling with a plan. Werner's bringing more men to Owens valley meant he was determined to get the water, no matter what the cost. As he sat on his saddle sipping from his cup, he stared at the fog. A plan to save the water seemed just as murky. Dynamite procured from Jonas, blowing up a meeting place somehow just didn't sit well with him. Besides, a meeting didn't have to be in a building. The roan a few feet away, munching on tall, very thick grass, was no help.

After two cups of the bitter brew, Stryker broke camp and saddled the unhelpful roan. An hour later, the sun poked its face through the clouds and as the day grew brighter. The seeds of a plan began to sprout. First, he had to ride to Cleo's ranch house and have a talk with Elfego.

Stryker arrived at the Gaines ranch house two hours later. He dismounted, pulled off the bridle, uncoiled the rope halter from around the saddle horn, and hitched the roan to the rail. He figured on a longer stay than his last visit. Might take a while to work out the details with Baca. Quiet, real quiet, and odd no one came out to greet him, he thought. Stryker drew the Peacemaker and stepped across the dirt entryway to the door. It hung slightly open. He leveled the Colt and pushed open the door with his left hand.

Whether he sprung to his right before the shot, after the shot, or at the same time, it's hard to say. Regardless, the bullet plowed through his hair less than an inch from his head, and Stryker let loose two quick rounds from the Colt as he leaped.

Shane took the first .44 round in his left shoulder. The second one blew off the bottom half of his right ear.

Shane recognized Stryker a half second after firing. Stryker's first bullet spun his torso left; otherwise Stryker's second shot would have punched him in the forehead. Shane, sitting on the floor still gripping the .32 revolver, clutched his shoulder. He pulled his hand away, dropped the gun, and grabbed the shoulder again.

Stryker straightened. He then realized the partially hidden body lying behind Shane was the boy's mother. He still held her hand.

"Cleo," Stryker said.

"Yes sir. She's dead." Shane's sobbing had dried up a half hour ago. Now he sat beside his mother, the finality of her death sinking in. "She was alive when I come in an' got to her. She reached for my hand and died." He stared at her face as he spoke, then looking up at Stryker he fought back more tears. "I don't think I can let go of her hand."

Stryker holstered the Peacemaker. "Where's Elfego?"

"Who?" Shane couldn't hold 'em back. Tears streamed down his face. They bubbled in his mouth as he spoke.

"Gunner, where is he?"

"He's gone. He ain't here."

Stryker walked closer. Cleo lay face down and he saw the blood. It pooled out from under her chest. She'd been shot. Her dress was crumpled up around the hips. He knelt and put his hand on the side of Cleo's neck. Shane was right. "Who shot her?"

Shane wiped his face on his sleeve. "I don't know," Shane snubbed.

"See anybody?"

"I see'd two men ridin', way off, way down the road. That's all.

"Your mother say anything 'fore she died?"

"Not really." Shane's eyes remained fixed on his mother's hand in his. Blood flowed down his arm and ran on her fingers.

"What you mean by that, kid?" Stryker pulled Shane's hand from his shoulder. The bullet hole was on the outside fleshy part of the boy's upper arm.

"Something like 'aa . . . ss . . . hh.'" Shane looked up at Stryker. "Don't make sense to me. Weren't nobody smokin' nothun'.

"Ashe," Stryker intoned.

"I guess so. Can you help me bury my ma?"

"We'll tend to that arm first." Stryker figured the youngster tried to help him in Libra's kitchen. Otherwise, his helping to put Cleo's body in a grave would've had less than a fifty percent chance. Stryker pulled Shane to his feet and pushed him toward the kitchen. The boy tried to hold on to his mother's hand, but when he saw her body dragging on the floor, he let go. "You gotta let go sometime, kid." But Stryker realized when he said it, Shane probably wouldn't ever let go–just like he hadn't.

He washed the arm wound with whiskey found in the kitchen cupboard and dressed it with bandages from the same cabinet. The whiskey burned when applied to arm and ear, but Shane gritted his teeth and didn't flinch. He was already practicing stoicism. And later, when Stryker tacked the boards together for a casket, dug a shallow grave, and put Cleo in it, Shane refused to cry.

By the time all that was completed, shadows were stretching eastward. "It'll be dark soon," Stryker told Shane. "We're going to town. Bring what you need to stay a few days." Even if Elfego showed, Stryker wanted the boy out of the way. A buckboard sat parked between the tool shed and the corral. He studied it for a bit. "Put the mule on the wagon."

Stryker let Shane struggle to harness the mule before stepping in to help. Stryker rode the roan in lead; Shane followed in the buckboard. Each rider wrestled with his own thoughts. It hadn't occurred to Stryker to console the boy. At one point along the way, Stryker pulled the roan over, allowing Shane to come along beside him. "Where'd Gunner go?"

"He went off to paint. Up in the mountains, that's what he said. Them ones." Shane pointed at the Sierras.

"Say when he'd be back?"

"Three days I think. He ain't always accurate, though."

Stryker reasoned if Elfego said three days, he wouldn't be going too far into the mountains, but who knows. Once Baca searched for the right landscape setting, he might keep trying to find a perfect scene farther and farther up the mountain. Stryker figured he had at least four days before the new men from Los Angeles made it to Bishop Creek. The Cavin fellow would be useful, seeing how he'd fought in the war, but Elfego's gun would not only be welcomed, it'd be needed. All right, when he got the kid settled, he'd take a day's ride and look for Baca.

"Why'd they kill my ma?"

Stryker shook his head.

"Why? She never done nothin' to nobody. You think they done somethin' to her, an' that's why they kilt her? So, she wouldn't tell nobody?" Shane asked.

"Let's go Shane."

"Wait Stryker. I wanna catch them men who done it." Shane's face suddenly turned dark. "An' I'm gonna kill 'em!"

The kid's outburst caused Stryker to flashback when his parents were murdered on Fisherman's Wharf. He'd been around twelve, like this boy. One of the thugs held him and made him watch while they slit the throats of his mother and father. He'd wanted to kill those men. He should have, and he always regretted that he didn't.

"Will you help me?"

"How long ago did Gunner show up at your home?"

Shane scrunched his face, thinking the question came at an odd time.

"I dunno, may two summers back. A year after my real Pa left I reckon." Then quickly adding, "He ain't no good shootin' an' fightin'. You are. I can tell. My ma thought so too."

"You'll be staying at a boarding house in town until Gunner gets back. We're going there now." *Not yet,* Stryker thought. *But you'll find out who Gunner is.*

Stryker spurred the roan. The boy would stay for the time being at Stella's. He halted and waited for Shane to come alongside again, "Shane, listen and do what I tell you. You might hear things around town, maybe even at where you're staying. You're to keep your mouth shut and do nothing 'til I or Gunner get back. Not a damn thing, understand? Even if you hear something about who murdered your ma, you don't say or do shit. Act like it means nothing. I'll tell the Stella woman you're my nephew. She know you?"

"Stella? I don't think so. I don't know her. Who is . . .?"

"She runs the boarding house. Do exactly what I say. You do that . . . I'll help you."

"You mean you'll help me kill 'em?"

"Yes." Stryker heeled the roan again.

Shane followed on the buckboard, his spirits lifted because a man, a man his mother aptly called a vicious killer, had agreed to help him. To a young boy–or to anyone for that matter–the prospect of going up against bad men with a man like Stryker, is . . . yes, comforting.

Stryker and Shane approached the edge of Bishop Creek a little past the normal dinner hour. The residual glow of the setting sun faded away, and nightfall claimed the evening. Stryker led them around the stables at the southern end of town and to the rear of Stella's boarding house.

"Stay here," Stryker said, climbing up the two back steps. He entered without knocking. The back door led directly into the kitchen. A swinging door, not like the bat wings of a saloon, but a single door hinged on one side separated the kitchen from the dining area where Stryker had supper with Councilman Ralston and three men, Ashe, R.J., and Texas. Texas, he knew would be missing, since he'd shoved the sai in the man's brains. Ralston wouldn't need to take a room, unless his wife put him in the doghouse, or he'd found other female company.

Regardless, when Stryker pushed through the swinging door, the dining room was empty.

Stryker searched downstairs and then upstairs. Stella was not to be found. The three upstairs rooms had their doors open, showing upstairs empty as well. *Shit.* He'd counted on having her watch the kid so he could track down that damn Elfego. He stepped out the front door and spotted the sign, "Be back in one hour."

Out back, Shane waited patiently by the roan and mule. Finally, after several minutes, Stryker came out. "Stella's not here, could be up to forty-five minutes. Come in. We'll wait."

"Wait for what?" Stella asked, rounding the back corner of the boardinghouse. She carried a full sack of groceries. "You want a room or just supper? Here." Stella practically threw the bag to Stryker. "Why you coming in the back? If you want dinner, you have to wait awhile. Didn't know they was so many folks a-wantin' supper tonight." She climbed the steps with some effort. "Well, come on in. There's two more a-comin'."

Stryker and Shane climbed the steps and entered the kitchen.

"Put 'em down there," Stella said. "I'll see if them other two showed up yet." She pushed open the swinging door, but stayed in the doorway.

Stryker set the bag on the counter and went to open the door wider in a move to go around her.

"The other two haven't showed up yet," Stella said, tying her apron on as Stryker side-stepped her.

He turned and saw Shane coming by her as well. "I need to make arrangements for the boy to stay awhile."

"By his-self?"

"I'll pay."

"We can talk about it later. I need ta get fixin' supper. Got coffee if ya want some, food'll be 'bout half hour."

"Shane, get the coffee," Stryker ordered. Growling in his belly signed its impatience for a meal. Stella needed to commence fixin'.

Stryker sipped from the cup Shane handed to him. Not in the mood to talk. Shane, who'd also gotten a cup for himself, sat beside Stryker and followed suit. It took longer than thirty minutes, but eventually, Stella burst through the swing door with two plates of sausages, biscuits, and gravy.

"I know it's like breakfast food, but I put it together quick–apple pie for dessert." Stella set the plates in front of them and went back into the kitchen. Stryker eagerly split a sausage with his fork and stuffed half in his mouth. He glanced over at Shane and noticed the boy toying with a gravy covered biscuit with his fork, but not eating.

"Better eat kid."

"I ain't hungry."

"Eat, dammit."

Shane forked a piece of biscuit and put it in his mouth. He chewed slowly and then swallowed. When he lowered his fork for another piece, Stryker ate the other half of his sausage.

Stryker heard the front door open and slam shut. Heavy boots pounded in the hallway, coming toward them–more than one pair. The boots started talking.

"Why'd you shoot her, Ashe. She was a good fuck. Bucked like crazy."

"We wuz told to. Shut up."

If Shane heard the man's name, he didn't act like it. He continued the slow, deliberate eating. Stryker cut into another piece of sausage and eyed the two men entering the dining room.

"Evening mister," Ashe said. He scrapped a chair back from the table opposite Stryker and Shane, and plopped down. R.J. sat as well. Neither man hung up his gun prior to sitting. "Didn't get your name last time," Ashe said.

"Stryker," He replied with a mouth full of sausage, and he cut into a biscuit.

Stella pushed though the swing door. "You're here. I'll get you some coffee. Your plates will be right out." She disappeared back into the kitchen.

"Who you got here with ya, mister Stryker?" R. J. forced a fake smile.

"Shane," Stryker answered, sopping the last piece of biscuit in the gravy. Shane kept his head lowered, working faithfully to eat the food on his plate.

Stella came out with two cups of coffee. She sat them in front of Ashe and R. J. Saying nothing, she spun to go back in the kitchen. She returned shortly with plates loaded with the food. "Here ya go." She noticed Stryker's empty plate. "Well, you was mighty hungry! I'll get your pie." And she picked up Stryker's plate. She left with it and reappeared with a large slice of peach pie. "The crust is a little burnt. Sorry, I hope you like it though."

Stryker tried the pie and realized Stella had been honest about the crust. He picked the pie up with his hand.

Ashe and R.J. hungrily launched into eating their own food. Both men busily cut into the sausages using a knife and fork.

Stryker shifted the pie to his left hand and took a bite. As he did, he pulled the Peacemaker and pointed it at Ashe. The first bullet plowed into the big man's chest, left of center, blasting him out of the chair. A surprised R.J. took Stryker's second shot, also in the chest.

A startled Shane suddenly looked across at the empty chairs. Both men lay on the floor, one was groaning. Shane starred up at Stryker, who was taking a second bite of pie. The boy's mouth was gaped open, a question on his face. "Why?"

Stryker kept chewing.

"Did they . . . Ma?"

Stryker nodded.

Shane laid his fork down and got up. He walked around the table and saw both men on the floor. R. J. was dead. Ashe lay on his side, groaning.

Shane walked over to Ashe and kicked his face.

Stella burst through the door. "What on earth . . .?"

"They killed his ma." Stryker shoved the last of the pie in his mouth.

"They killed his ma? Why? Did they . . . her?"

"Yes."

The overweight woman ran around the table, got next to Shane, and kicked.

Stryker wiped his mouth with his hand. "When you two finish kicking, we need to load 'em in the wagon. The other'n dead?"

"Yes," Stella said, "and this one just died too."

"Let's load 'em up." Stryker got up from the table.

"You two better go on outta here too," Stella said, pulling Shane away from Ashe's body. "I'll clean up what blood there is and sweep the wagon tracks out back."

"Give me a hand Shane," Stryker said. Stryker took the shoulders. Stella and Shane, the legs, and they carried the bodies to the wagon.

Stryker, standing by the wagon with Shane, dug out two-dollar gold pieces and gave them to Stella, who'd just finished hugging the boy. "The pie was good," he said, placing the money in her hand.

"You don't owe me." Stella tried to give back the money.

"Keep it."

Shane climbed in the wagon. Stryker got on the roan. They started down the alley.

Stella cleaned the blood off the floor and swept out the wagon tracks. When asked later about the gunshots, she replied she hadn't heard them and that they must have come from another house. She'd *spilled* coffee on where she cleaned up the bloodstains and put a rug down on the opposite side of the table. Suspicious, the sheriff noticed the rug which looked out of place, and when he found nothing under it, he left.

Stryker led Shane away from town, and toward where Poenabe and Paya had been hanged, but stayed out of the trees. They dumped the bodies of Ashe and R.J. Stryker figured coyotes and other predators would be grateful. Stryker maintained a steady pace and conversation between man and boy was limited to the brief pause when they stopped to piss.

"Thank you, Mister Stryker," Shane said.

"I had other reasons for killing 'em." Stryker'd been thinking about who told Ashe to kill Cleo. He'd heard Ashe talking about it at Stella's. Most likely Ralston. He should have gotten that out of Ashe before he shot him. A mistake, he'd let avenging the woman's murder for Shane cloud his judgement. Ah, what the hell, he might get the opportunity to *question* Ralston later.

In another two hours, Stryker and Shane saw the waning firelight of the Righteous Sisters' camp in the distance. As they got closer, they spotted a solitary figure sitting by the fire. Eula.

It wouldn't be as comfortable as a bed at Stella's, but Stryker figured they could throw a bedroll under one of the wagons and at least have uninterrupted sleep til sun up.

"Stryker!" Eula exclaimed, relieved when she recognized the man riding into their camp. "I'sa wondering where you been. Who's that you got wit ya?" She rose to greet them as they dropped to the ground and walked into better light.

"The boy's Shane." Stryker helped himself to a cup of coffee and squatted by the fire. Need you to watch over him while I go find his father." He left out news of Cleo's death for now. "I'll be heading out at daybreak."

Hany and Jemima clamored out of the wagon. "Stryker!" Jemima yelled, mimicking Eula. Hany followed, but had the good sense not to repeat another greeting.

"And this is Shane," Eula said. She put a gentle arm around his shoulders. A sixth sense told her things weren't right about the boy. "He's stayin' wit us for a while. It'll be good to have a man around here again, won't it girls?"

"It shore will, it most shorely will." Jemima sounded as if she really meant it.

"The Paiutes came by," Hany interjected. They found Poenabe and Paya."

The mood turned somber. "Who you think woulda done that, Stryker?" Eula asked, dropping her arm from Shane.

"Not sure," Stryker said. "Coulda been . . ."

"An' we killed 'em!" Shane declared.

"Maybe, like I said, coulda been a couple men we met earlier tonight." Stryker sipped from the cup.

"An' they killed my ma too." Shane toned it down, almost to a mumble.

"Your ma?" She put her arm around Shane again.

"Yes." Shane's eyes welled up. He fought hard, but Eula's mothering broke down his defenses.

"You poor thing," Jemima lamented, and threw her arm around the boy's waist.

Shane really struggled now.

"You boys hungry?" Hany asked.

"We ate," Stryker said. "C'mon Shane, let's tend to the horses.

The women released their embraces, encouraging Shane to do something to take his mind off his ma. He stumbled after Stryker, wiping his eyes. Stryker was quick with the roan. When he'd laid the saddle by the fire and secured the horse on a picket line, he went to help Shane.

"Gunner say where on the mountain?" Stryker asked again.

"No, he just rode off following the creek toward 'em, pulling a mule on a rope."

The women had all crawled into the wagon by the time Stryker and Shane finished their chores. The two bedded down under the Righteous Sister's wagon. Stryker fell asleep listening to low murmurings overhead and the boy's sniffing.

Stryker rolled from under the wagon before sun rise. He rekindled the fire and saddled the roan while coffee boiled. Only Eula got up to see him off.

"When you be back," she asked, holding onto the roan's bridle as Stryker booted the stirrup.

"A day, or two at the most. The revival's over." He reverted to asking questions with statements.

"Yeah, it's done ended, but I dunno if'n we'da still sang anyway, Elvin kilt."

"I don't know if the boy's father will show up at their place 'fore I return. Don't go down there now. Take the boy and the wagons up to Laws. There's a woman named Libra lives on the western edge of town. Tell her I said for all of you to stay by her house, quarter mile away. Tell her Cleo's dead. Don't let her take the kid in. Keep him with you."

With that Stryker heeled the roan and rode off in the dark.

Eula returned to the fire and poured herself a cup of coffee.

CHAPTER TWELVE

The sun had been an hour above the White Mountains by the time he passed the Gaines' house and tracked beside the creek toward the Sierras.

It wasn't much to go on, but if the wanna-be artist, Elfego, wanted a water scene for his *masterpiece*, then maybe the creek might lead to a small lake or pond up on the mountain, one scenic enough to paint. Stryker thought Baca will have to realize who he is and what he is. He's no fucking artist. He's a gun-toting lawman. *The fool–can't put stripes on a mule and call it a zebra.*

Any feint trace of a trail played out in a couple of miles and Stryker only had the creek to follow. He'd give himself two days. If he couldn't find Baca and persuade him to come down off the mountain without his art tablets by then, he'd go it alone.

Late the same day Stryker gained elevation, and when he looked back toward Bishop Creek in the distance, it lay a thousand feet below. Soon his view of town was blocked after he'd rounded a series of hills, and moraines as he worked his way higher. He came to what appeared to be a mining trail that snaked farther ahead into aspen trees. The trail led away from the creek, but he took it. Upon reaching the aspens, he came to another creek, called Horton Creek but unknown to Stryker. He had to rest the roan more often now, even walking and leading the big horse. Towering off to his right the thirteen-thousand-foot Mount Tom, treeless and crowned in rocky shale, loomed over the valley. Straight ahead in the distance, the mountains sagged lower forming a saddle before climbing back up to the thirteen-thousand-foot Basin Mountain on his left. Looking farther up the trail, Stryker saw it climbed through a series of switchbacks. He figured he must have climbed over five-thousand feet already and should near ten-thousand feet. That and the switchbacks convinced him to make camp for the night. He dropped from the trail, closer to the steam where the roan would have water and tall grass. The air turned cold when the sun went down, and he built a fire in front of a large gray boulder to reflect its warmth. He made the fire bigger than normal too. The last thing on his mind after a plate of beans and hot coffee, and before he curled up in the blanket, was that tomorrow he would ride higher until noon and turn back.

Cold, that's what it was when he rolled out of the blanket, blankets actually. He'd rolled up in his bedroll and the saddle blanket. A few leaves on the quakies had yellowed even though it was only late summer. Fall at this elevation would arrive before long. Thankfully, sticks he scrounged up for the fire were dry, and it didn't take much coaxing to get a blaze going again. He boiled hot water for coffee and saved some water to boil a potato. He ate it with the rest of the beans. One good thing about being high up on the east side of the mountain, the sun hits early. He kept the wool jacket on when he saddled the roan and started up toward the switchbacks.

After about an hour, he emerged from the switchbacks, and upon cresting the last incline Stryker arrived at Horton Lake. Tall pressed pines spiraled skyward in the lush grass surrounding the lake. A few stands of quaking aspen trees also staked out claims along the lake shore. The lake itself was roughly a quarter mile long and a little over an eighth mile wide. Water, clear and cold, filled the lake from snow runoff. It was a beautiful picture, and Elfego sat on the south end of the lake painting.

Stryker heeled the roan, pulled the reins slightly leftward, and pressed his right knee inward. He acted deliberately, took his time, rode slowly. He had given little thought to what he would say to Baca, informing him of Cleo's death. He'd focused on persuasion, convincing the young gunman to join with the ranchers, protecting the water. Now, Stryker realized the two matters were related. He didn't give much of a shit about Baca's love life, but he wanted his help. He must be tactful. Fuck, he didn't know how to be tactful.

"Howdy Stryker. What you doing way up here?" Baca lay his brush aside and stood up from the wooden folding chair. The broad grin tempered by a furrowed brow.

Stryker leaned forward, resting his elbows on the saddle horn. He eyed Elfego's work on the easel. The lake, the mountains, and the sky, were simply plastered on the canvas, but with no imagination, no sense of depth, no emotion. *Damn, Baca, can't you see you can't paint worth a shit?*

"Need your help."

"My help? Doing what?" The grin slid off his Baca's face.

"Your gun."

Baca's countenance darkened.

Stryker dismounted. He walked past Elfego without an effort to shake hands or show any other sign of a friendly greeting and stood in front of the easel. "This is shit."

"You shouldn't go on so. Your effusive praise is embarrassing," Baca drawled dryly. He got a little irritated.

"Los Angeles is sending up a bunch of men to seize the water in the valley. I intend to stop 'em. I'll need your help."

"I may not be much of an artist, but that is what I am now. Cleo ain't gonna have a shootin' man in her house, especially with her boy. She's the first woman I ever had who'd have me. Ain't gonna fuck it up."

"Elfego, she knows you're no God-damn artist. I heard her say it. Drop the bull-shittin'. Not impressin' her with it. She'd rather have a real man in her bed, not a silly fool like Gunner. Besides, she's dead."

"She ain't dead! You lyin' son-o-bitch!" Baca lowered his head and charged at Stryker like a bull.

Baca's attack, even though strengthened with adrenaline'd rage, was no match against the considerable fighting skills of the mixed-breed. Stryker sidestepped him and shoved a boot on Elfego's hip as he ran past.

The force of the kick deflected Baca's momentum and sent him sprawling on the ground. Stryker was on him in an instant, the sai drawn. Before Elfego could throw a punch, Stryker gripped Baca's throat with one hand and shoved the sai in his mouth.

"Cleo's dead." Stryker growled through gritted teeth, mustering all the compassion he could–which was none, actually. And then he tactfully added, "I shot the men who killed her."

Stryker's words finally got through to Elfego. The sai pricking the back of his throat helped Stryker get his point across. Baca dropped his arms. He nodded his head, but the tip of the sai bit deeper, and he lay still.

Stryker withdrew the weapon and stood up. Elfego rolled over and got to his feet, spitting blood.

"Why'd they kill her?" Baca spit a mouthful of blood and saliva.

"The water. She wrote the senator. She was fightin' for it."

Baca studied Stryker briefly. "How'd she die?"

"Shot her and . . ." Stryker held off more, being tactful again.

"And what?" Elfego asked, "They raped her?"

"Reckon so."

"The boy?"

"Okay, left him with the Righteous Sisters, those negro gospel singers."

"All right, what you want me to do?"

Baca packed rapidly. The two men were on the trail back to town in less than ten minutes. On the way, Stryker told Baca of his plan. Baca left the easel and painting materials in place.

The ride down went more swiftly than the ride up the mountain, and they made it back to the outskirts of Bishop Creek shortly before dark. Baca insisted on seeing Shane first. They veered away from reaching town and rode to Law's.

When he recognized them approaching in the waning daylight, Shane ran out to greet Baca and Stryker. "Gunner!" Shane yelled as he ran. He stopped short and allowed Baca to close the gap. Baca reached down and swung the boy up behind him. Shane wrapped his arms around Baca's waist. "They killed ma."

"I know, son. Stryker told me," Baca said. No more words passed between them until Shane leapt down without help, and Baca dismounted. The Righteous Sisters stood back a way, between the campfire and the Conestoga, allowing the men to talk in private. Baca knelt on one knee in front of Shane.

"Sorry about your ma," Baca began. "If I hadn't been so stupid, I'd-a been here to stop it. I can't bring her back, but now I'm gonna help carry on what your ma was trying to do. She'd want me to, don't you think?" Shane nodded once, his eyes watering. "I need you to stay with these ladies for now. Will you do that for me–for your ma too?"

"Yes," Shane said reluctantly.

"Another thing, Shane." Now it was Baca who sounded uncertain. "My name ain't Gunner."

"It ain't?" Shane asked, scrunching his face and looking confused.

"My name's Elfego Baca." Your ma never knew.

"Why didn't you tell ma?"

"Thought she's same as Libra, not wanting guns around, an' all. I was hoping she'd like me more. Guess I was wrong, though. Shane, some things are worth fightin' for. That's what I gonna do now."

"But Gunner, uh, Elfugo . . . you ain't no good shootin'. Ma told me."

"It's Elfego, and I . . ." Baca fumbled with explaining the lie he'd been living.

"Baca is sheriff over in New Mexico. He can handle a gun, and I need him," Stryker said.

"Stryker's right. It's true. Now I'm gonna go with 'im. You stay here and I'll be back soon." Baca rose to his feet. "All right, Stryker, let's go."

"Where we headed now, Stryker?" Baca asked as they rode away.

"Hardware store."

Stryker filled in Baca about Law's business partners, Jonas and Milford. He also told him about how he planned to use them and whoever they'd manage to recruit. And then he added, "And we need more bullets."

Stryker and Baca pulled up in front of the Laws Mercantile and Dry Goods store. No lights shone inside, but Stryker dismounted, wrapped the reins on a rail, and pounded on the entry door. Baca dismounted too when he realized Stryker would eventually beat down the door. Finally, a lantern lit.

"We ain't open! Come back in the morning!" Came an irritated shout on the other side of the door.

"It's Stryker. Open up."

The dead bolt slid open. The door cracked open two inches. Stryker shoved it wider, knocking Jonas out of the way.

"Jesus, Stryker! You could'a let me let me open the door." One look at Stryker's face stopped the storekeeper from further protestations.

"How many men you get?" Stryker demanded.

"Six, counting me and Milford," Jonas replied, with trepidation.

"Shit, you got six out of the whole fucking valley. Bunch of cowardly women in this town; you *should* lose your God-damned water!" Stryker's anger on full display.

"Two of 'em *are* women." Jonas backed farther from the door.

"Four men and two women? That's all you got?" Baca came in and stood beside the furious mixed-breed. "Jesus H. Christ."

"We got lots o' wagons and horses," Jonas added. "Hello, Gunner."

"Will the horses shoot?" Baca asked.

"Go get 'em," Stryker ordered.

"The horses? Now?" It's getting kinda late, Jonas whined.

"The four. Do it now, Jonas," Stryker growled.

"What's happening?" Milford heard talking and came down the steps in his nightgown. "Everything all right?"

"The two men and two women, get 'em over here." Stryker shoved Jonas aside.

"Now?" Milford asked.

Stryker sprang on Milford, grasped his throat, and drove him against the wall. With eyes glinting as steel slits, he snarled, "Jonas has ten minutes to save your ass."

"I'll be right back." Jonas dashed out the front door.

"Get four boxes of .44-40 shells." Stryker released Milford's throat. "Two for me, two for him." Stryker dipped his head sideways at Baca.

"Jonas," The man walking beside Jonas struggled to keep pace. The other three rode on the buckboard, a man flanked by two women on the seat. "You told me one's Gunner, what's the other man like?"

"Ain't likable, named Stryker's half Mex or Chinaman I reckon.

"Other half white?"

"Rattlesnake."

Turned out the two men and two women were married couples. The women had volunteered first, shaming their husbands into joining the fight. Stryker thought about shooting the four men and just using the women. He was wondering if the water got to southern California, if it would turn the men there into pussies too. Eight against two dozen, shit.

The first man in the door started to say, "We hear'd folks been gettin' killed and . . ."

Stryker turned to face him.

"An' they're just building an irrigation system." The second man finished the first man's sentence before he got inside.

"This is Mister Wagner," Jonas said to Stryker. Jonas put his hand behind Wagner's back and shoved him toward Stryker

"Call me Saul." Saul stuck out his hand. Stryker ignored it. "Gunner," Saul said, throwing a nod at him.

"I'm Rolf." The second man took a step forward and offered a half-hearted salute–also ignored.

"Four. Get the other two," Stryker said.

Saul reversed to the doorway, cupped a hand by his mouth, and called out, "Honey, you and Sophie wanna come in now?"

Stryker noted Saul asked.

"This is my wife, Angel. Angel, this is Mister Stryker." Saul gestured to Stryker as if seeking approval from her. Angel, a large, stout woman with a stern demeanor, could eat Cleveland.

"I'm Sophie." A smaller, less imposing woman, who may have only nibbled at a tiny town, offered a tilted head dip. Sophie's stiffness may have been part facade, perhaps hiding a friendlier side. Angel was genuine drill sergeant.

"You ladies know how to shoot?" Baca interrupted, sensing Stryker was close to punching somebody.

"Pistols, rifles, shotguns, just about anything that shoots," Angel declared.

Stryker believed the woman. "Jonas, make sure everybody has one of each and plenty of ammunition." Stryker recounted a general outline of the plan. He left out a few details, like–it had little chance of working, a lot depended on what the L.A. crowd did. And once the shooting ended, if indeed it actually started, some of them would likely be killed. "I'll ride out to Libra's and survey the ground around the house tonight. Elfego, ride with me. We meet back here at nine in the morning." Finished, Stryker walked out of the store. Baca followed, closing the door behind him.

The six people left in the store had plenty of questions they'd wanted to ask Stryker. None dared ask. Saul queried the other five, "What do you suppose he'd do if we don't show up in the morning?"

"He'll kill us," Milford said.

"That man didn't ride in here cause he wanted to save us or the water. He came here to do a job. How he does it, and who he kills, don't matter to him," Angel said, staring pensively at the closed door.

"How d'you come by that?" Jonas asked.

"Cleo told me. She said he's a hired killer the senator sent."

"Cleo? How'd she find out?" Jonas asked further, with a puzzled expression. "And, a senator, what senator?"

"George Hearst, Cleo wrote him, asked for help here to save our water." Angel glared hard at Jonas. "I like him."

"One thing I don't understand," Sophie said, canting her head. "Why'd he call Gunner, Elfego?"

Stryker wanted to inspect outside Libra's house at night. He'd come back in the morning for another look see prior to the nine o'clock meeting. "That's enough for tonight, Elfego," Stryker said, after they'd walked the grounds for the better part of an hour discussing strategy. "Heading to the livery."

"Reckon I'll go in and tell Libra about Cleo," Baca allowed. He drew in a long breath and released it, implying an unpleasant task ahead.

Stryker figured that meant Elfego would provide Libra with full service consoling. "See you here at eight." He swung the reins across the roan's mane, guiding it toward Laws Livery at the far edge of town. The hired guns from Los Angeles would show up soon, maybe on the noon train tomorrow. Werner won't wait long, Stryker figured. Word about town on the meeting at Libra's had likely found its way to the commissioner's ears by now. How deadly were Werner's intentions? His own plan depended on that. He needed the L.A. bunch all together. Risky, but trying to take them out one at a time, was even more so. He'd stable the roan, and get a good night's rest for himself too.

Stryker stabled the horse. Whoever tended the livery had gone home. He gave it water and then cleaned and brushed the roan as it munched oats and hay from the trough. Once he'd cared for the animal, he threw the saddle and bedding down in the next stall and got some much-needed sleep.

The stable door rolled open while still dark outside. Stryker woke with a jerk. He realized he'd slept soundly; again, no bad dreams, no dreams at all. He rose, strapped on the Peacemaker, and stepped from the stall.

"Waaaeee!" The boy in his teens screamed like a girl.

"Easy kid. Light a lantern," Stryker said.

"Whoa shit. You scared shit outta me."

Stryker thought the kid's speech sounded a little odd. When the lantern flame flickered to life, he saw why. The boy's front teeth were missing. "You're working in Laws now."

"Oh, it's you!" Dillon said, sounding relieved. "I got the living shit kicked out of me there. Moved back up here to Laws yesterday. Hey, that man doin' the kickin' wuz wantin' to know all 'bout you! I didn't tell 'im nothin', honest." Dillon eased a step backward.

"I know that. Obliged."

"He beat me so hard, gave hisself a stroke 'an died from it."

"I killed him," Stryker said.

"You? What? How? Weren't no marks on 'im. Sheriff said he stroked an' bled to death. I thought he wore hisself out on me." Dillon had doubts.

Stryker whipped the sai from his back. He flipped the tines up and said, "Rammed it up his nose."

"Fu—ck. That musta' hurt."

Stryker returned the weapon to the pouch in his back. "Did me a favor, keeping your mouth shut. I returned it. Want you to do something else."

"Yes . . . sir," Dillon agreed, sounding a little hesitant.

"First, tell me about this Ralston man, Councilman in Bishop Creek."

"Don't know a lot. He married good, money I mean. Her pa's rich. See'd him drinkin' some–the councilman."

"Where do I find him?"

"He comes to the livery down in Bishop Creek, an' borrows a buggy on Mondays–ever Monday morning." Dillon sensed he might keep his remaining teeth and breathed a little easier.

"Where's he take it?"

"Here, I guess. Poenabe, a friend, I guess he's a friend. He's a Paiute, half o' one, I reckon. We go fishin' an'."

"Ralston and the buggy, kid." Stryker's patience thinned.

"Uh yeah, Poenabe said he meets the train here. Picks up a woman an' they go ridin' together. He don't meet her at tha train, he says. Waits out back, out back there, I think." Dillon pointed a forefinger around his body toward rear of the stable. Hey, today's Monday, ain't it?" Dillon dashed to the back door and peeked outside. "He ain't there. Figures, train ain't due til noon." Dillon hurriedly wiped the sheepish grin from his face.

"There'll be a meeting at Libra's house tonight. Everyone fighting Los Angeles over the water will be there. Spread the word, especially at the hotel in Bishop where the men from L.A. are staying. Make sure they know. Do it this morning. And Dillon, keep your damn mouth shut about me."

"Yes, sir," Dillon said, cupping a hand over his nose.

Stryker saddled the roan and led it out of the stall. "Go. Get your ass down there talking about the meeting."

"Yes sir." Dillon stood aside as Stryker led the roan down the center aisle and out of the stable.

Stryker climbed on the roan. The plan had just gotten a little better, because he now had more control. He rode to Libra's. The big cottonwood out back of the house was the only large tree, only smaller ones on the sides and front. The front of her house faced the street and not the center of town. A dry creek bed ran roughly parallel to the street, some fifty yards beyond it on the other side. After a couple hundred yards, the dry creek veered away and found its way to a wet stream, the one which flowed through Bishop Creek. During a hard rain the creek bed had water in it, but it hadn't rained in a week. Stryker continued around the house, and he saw no other natural features. He still had an hour before the nine o'clock meeting so he tethered the roan in back under the cottonwood and entered the rear door without knocking. He suspected Elfego might have worked up an appetite during the night and needed a hardy breakfast.

Yep.

"Morning Stryker," Baca said. He'd seen Stryker riding around the house and was not surprised when he came through the door. "Want some breakfast? Libra's tidying up the house. Got biscuits and gravy here." Baca pointed his fork at the plate of biscuits and a gravy bowl on the table. "Ham on the stove. Help yourself. Coffee in the pot there too." He pointed his fork at the stove. "Find what you want outside?"

Stryker grabbed a plate and filled it. Did the same with a cup. He sat, cut into the ham, then said, "It'll do."

Baca allowed breakfast conversation over. He stuffed the last half of a gravy-dripping biscuit in his mouth.

"Why, Mister Stryker," Libra said, bursting into the kitchen. "Want some break-? Uh, see you got it already." She poured her coffee and sat.

"Need your house tonight," Stryker said, meaning Libra. "Better if you're not here."

Libra looked at Baca with a question on her face. "Ohhh?"

"What for? Gunner, you know I don't allow guns, so if . . ." Libra pleaded her case to the man who might listen.

"My name's not Gunner, Libra. It's Elfego, Elfego Baca."

"Who the fuck are you two?"

"Cleo's dead." Baca had neglected to tell Libra that small bit of news too.

"Dead? Oh, my God! What's going on here?" Libra planted the cup on the table, spilling coffee on her shaky hand.

"It's the water," Stryker said.

"I don't understand. What's that have to do with Cleo?" Libra asked. "Someone kill her?"

"The water's to die for," Stryker offered, dryly.

"The men from Los Angeles or them in cahoots with 'em here, they shot her," Baca explained. "I'm gonna make 'em pay." Baca's face turned dark. "Some in Laws are helping me, this man here is too." Baca nodded at Stryker.

"Cleo wrote San Francisco, asked for help, for other ranchers too." Stryker pushed back from the table and stood. "Reason I'm here."

"And you Elfego, or whatever your name is, why are you in Laws?"

"Escaping my past, or trying to. I was a sheriff in New Mexico."

"A Sheriff," Libra repeated.

"Yeah," Baca confirmed.

"You can't paint," Libra said.

"Well, I . . ."

"No, you really can't paint. Just wanted you to know I'm not stupid," Libra huffed. She turned to Stryker. "When you want me out?"

"Hour before sundown," Stryker told her. "Let's go Baca." Stryker dug two bits from his pocket and dropped it on the table.

Elfego, sensing more explanation futile, followed Stryker out the back door.

Ten people waited in Laws Hardware for Stryker and Baca. "We got four more men to join us, Stryker," Jonas said, when they walked through the door. The four young men Jonas meant were Dillon and three others who didn't seem much older than sixteen, but each held a shotgun, a carbine repeater, and had a revolver stuck in the waist of his pants. Stryker thought they looked comfortable holding the long guns, maybe they'd hunted. All four answered yes when Baca asked them if they knew how to use the weapons.

Stryker went over the plans again, including the new part Stryker now had for Councilman Ralston. "Remember when to start shooting, and make the first shots with shotguns," Stryker growled. "Do exactly what I say, and some of you might stay alive."

Stryker walked from the store wondering how many of the ten would see another day. He didn't dwell on it too much, though. He really didn't care.

"You think he's serious?" One boy asked. "About staying alive, I mean."

"Them ain't laugh lines on 'im," Jonas snorted.

Stryker estimated an hour and a half before Ralston showed. He was thinking of something to do until Baca caught up to him.

"I told 'em if they failed to show up you'd shoot 'em." Elfego chuckled as he said it. "I half think you would." Baca got no reply from the mixed-breed, and then he figured maybe fifty percent was too low.

"What you doing til tonight?" Baca asked.

"Staying out of sight at the livery. You don't have to."

"Reckon I'll keep outta sight too." Baca reversed step and headed to Libra's.

Stryker found an empty stall with fresh straw and lay in it. He pulled the Stetson over his face, but he didn't sleep. He thought about Leigh. Times like these when he knew his life might end soon, made him think of her. Foolish he knew, but she probably came into his head because he always hoped he'd see her again. Hope—he clung to it, yet he loathed it. A distinct character trait of the man, one of the few which defined him, other than ruthless, violent, or just plain mean, was that *reason* shaped his thinking. But, he allowed himself this one fanciful delusion. Maybe that's why he was fearless in a fight, the prospect of death failed to bother him as it did others. Reflexes reacted with cool efficiency—

survival by animal instinct. He stood on the sharp edge, one side life, the other death. Didn't matter.

"Mister Stryker." Dillon stood by the open stall door. "There's a buggy coming."

Stryker, so deeply lost in an hour's worth of daydreaming, hadn't heard the boy enter the stable, and inwardly cursed himself for his failure. *Dammit.* He snatched the hat from his face and sprang to his feet. Striding quickly to the rear of the stable, he unlatched the back door and cracked it open. Ralston, in a one-horse doctor's buggy, crept slowly up Bishop Creek road toward Laws about three-hundred yards away. Stryker waited until the four-wheeled carriage pulled past him inside the door and parked at the back corner of the livery.

Snorting from the horse provided sound cover. Stryker opened the door. He stepped around to the far side of the buggy. Ralston leaned forward in the seat. Peeking around the corner of the building, he failed to see Stryker come up on his blind side. Ralston felt the buggy sway, when Stryker climbed in.

"Hey!" The councilman bellowed. "What are you . . .?" The barrel of the Peacemaker punched hard in his ribs.

"Shut up. Swing around. Drive away from town," Stryker ordered. A quick glance at the killer's eyes kept Ralston's protest in his throat.

"Where we going?" He finally asked. They'd gone roughly two miles south of Laws when Ralston gambled the question. "You gonna shoot me?" he squeaked.

"Take that trail," Stryker said, pointing a forefinger. The Colt remained in the man's ribs. "When you come to one heading north, take it." In a mile and a half, they came to another trail, one used by cattle drovers by-passing Laws. Ralston swung the horse north. Hoof marks left in the mud from the cattle herds made the trail badly rutted. After three bumpy miles, Stryker had Ralston turn back east. Eventually, they came to the main road heading south into Laws. "Take it," Stryker said.

Ralston breathed a little easier, thinking if the man beside him meant to kill him, he'd be dead already.

In a half hour, Libra's house, appeared in the distance. As they approached within a couple hundred yards, Stryker instructed Ralston,

"Put the buggy behind that house." Libra's house stood isolated at the north end of town, and Ralston had no trouble knowing which house Stryker meant.

"Get out." Stryker scooted out of the buggy on the same side with Ralston, keeping the Peacemaker snug against the man's ribs. They entered through the back door to the kitchen. "Sit down." There they waited, with Stryker sitting across the table, his gun cocked and pointed at Ralston's heart. After a while, Libra wandered into the kitchen.

She expressed little surprise at finding Stryker and Ralston in her house. Perhaps she'd already had enough surprises that morning and became inured to them. "Gunner, or Elfego, whoever, went to find you. You want coffee?"

"Get some rope," Stryker said.

"Would leather strappings do? I've got some hanging on the hitch rail."

"Soak 'em in the trough first."

Ralston waited until Libra left out the back door. "What are you gonna do with me?"

"Depends on your friends from Los Angeles. If they show up, you make a speech." Stryker kept the Colt pointed at Ralston's chest.

"If they don't come?" The councilman nerves bothered him again.

"They'll come, then I'll tell you what to say." Stryker said. "Right now, you'll tell me where Werner and Books are." Stryker squinted with one eye and sighted in on Ralston's forehead.

"You want Werner and Books, mister?" Ralston put the pieces together. "You're right. Them two are up to no good. They tricked us. We thought they came here to help with the irrigation. They're tryin' to steal our water!" He was talking fast now. Ralston stared at the end of the Peacemaker's barrel. "They stay at the Bishop Hotel. They meet there. Want me to take you?"

Libra flung open the kitchen door. "Here ya are. This enough?" She held out three long straps and let them hang to the floor.

"Tie his wrists behind the chair with one. Loop it through the slats."

When Libra finished securing the wrists, Stryker holstered the Colt and picked up the second strap off the table. He threw a slip knot around

Ralston's throat, and tied the loose end down at the wrist binding, tight. He used the third strap to secure each ankle to a rear leg chair so that Ralston's legs were bent backward at the knees.

"This leather's gonna shrink." Ralston said.

Stryker dragged the man and chair down the hall to the front room. He placed him by the front door, facing it, but for enough away so the door could open.

"There you are!" Baca yelled, rushing down the hall from the kitchen. "I been looking all over for you. What's he doing here?" Elfego pulled up short upon seeing the trussed-up councilman in the living room.

"Watch him. Shoot his balls if he moves. I figure he gave the order to kill Cleo. Be back shortly."

Stryker rode the buggy back to the stable. He left it parked where Ralston usually waited for his paramour. A prostitute from Virginia City, he'd sampled the charms of a few there, he might even know this one, *as in the biblical sense,* he mused to himself. But he didn't wait around to find out. He entered the livery, pulled the Winchester off the roan, and left out the front, heading across the street to the hardware store.

Jonas and Milford stood inside by the counter, with Jonas berating Milford when Stryker pushed through the door, and slammed it behind him. Jonas cut short the haranguing. "Stryker, and, how are you? Can we help you with . . .?"

"Ralston, Councilman from Bishop Creek, you know 'im."

"Yes, we know him," Jonas said.

"Not well, but we know him," Milford added. "Don't trust the bastard."

"Spread the word toward dusk, prior to the meeting at Libra's, that he's been kidnapped and being held at Libra's house."

"What are we . . .?" Jonas began.

"Do it," Stryker cut in. "Milford, ride to Bishop Creek. Tell it to the L.A. commissioner and that Books fellow with 'im–they're staying at the Bishop Hotel. If they're not there, find 'em and tell it to them directly. Then get your ass back here." Stryker turned back to Jonas. "Any questions on tonight."

"We ride over right after dark, go through the house and out back. Hide by the big cottonwood tree down at the road. We wait for 'em to show, then take our positions. Simple enough, I think."

"I'll be at Libra's til then," Stryker said, and walked out.

"Stryker!" A deep throated male called his name.

Stryker waited for Cavin to walk up the boardwalk.

"It's all over, Stryker," the cattleman huffed. "I just came from seein' that damn L.A. bastard at the Bishop Creek Hotel. He said we're sellin' out."

"Got bad news for him. His room number." Stryker said.

"Four. The other man with him's in five. Stryker, they're gonna sign the town water over, Laws *and* Bishop. We're too late." Cavin sounded exasperated. "And all the other ranchers are sellin'. They paid big money to all of Bishop Creek, my ranch too. All legal, he told me. Eminent domain or some shit. I feel like shootin' the sons o' bitches."

"Cavin, there'll be a meeting in Libra's house at dusk. Be there. Bring a shotgun."

When Stryker arrived at Libra's house, he saw Ralston had had the shit beat out of him. A blood-stained rolling pin lay near him on the floor. His face all bloody and swollen, teeth missing and nose flattened, the man barely remained conscious. "Need him to talk later," Stryker said.

"Libra took the rolling pin to him," Baca drawled.

"Fucker!" Libra spat. The two men understood–three actually. Ralston understood too. "He claimed it was Werner," Libra said, fire coming from her eyes. "That shitass really gave the order?" She reached for the rolling pin again.

"Coffee still good." Stryker headed to the kitchen.

Baca motioned for Libra to follow Stryker into the kitchen. "I'll watch him," Baca said. "See about the coffee."

Libra strolled past Stryker sitting at the table. Stopping by the stove, she placed a hand on the side of the coffee pot. "It's still warm."

"Pour it."

Libra filled two cups, gave one to Stryker, and sat. "She was my only cousin. We were very close." Her eyes grew moist. She slowly turned the cup on the table. "You got any family, Stryker?"

"No."

"So, you ain't married, I guess." Libra shifted her attention to Stryker. "Ever been?"

Stryker felt the old resentment rising in him. It happened when people tried to dig into his past. His face darkened. His eyes narrowed.

Libra changed the subject. "What you gonna do with that man in there?"

"If someone else doesn't kill him tonight, I will," Stryker said. "You should be leaving soon."

"Libra rose from the table. "I'll get ready."

Stryker remained sitting. Baca came in once, for two cups of water. Two hours passed. Libra's question brought back the memories. It was why he recoiled when she asked if he'd been married. He knew they would come. Damn. He'd prided himself on control–self-control, self-discipline. That's how he lived his life. He tried to hold back the memories, good and bad, but they came on anyway. During the day, he usually suppressed them. At night, they invaded the dreams, turning them into nightmares. The dreams kept happening, not so many lately. Strange . . . why not? Morgan? Still, they did come. Different, yet always the same, Leigh bloodied and dying. He'd been showing off his artillery skills. That's what killed her, his fault. He held her as she died that day. Leigh looked at him, trusting and loving, and said his name with her last breath.

"Aaahhh!" His own voice surprised him. The sound of it brought him back to the present. The bedroom door opened. Libra came out.

"You called for me?" She asked. She stood before him for a moment and then sat at the table. Her hair had been cut. It now hung only to her shoulders, straight and parted. She'd brushed her cheeks with make-up and put on lipstick. *Where'd she get the make-up?* Gone was the long dress. The skirt barely covered her knees. One couldn't deny it. The woman looked pretty good. "Baca told me of your plans here tonight. He said you'll be here when the others leave, you, Baca, and Ralston. So, I'm staying too. You'll need someone to load your guns."

They heard the wagons pulling up outside. Wagons and buggies, all parked allowing clear vision to the front door. Jonas remembered. That's a good sign, Stryker thought. Maybe they'll do the rest too like he told them. Dark now, lamps were lit inside all throughout the house. Two of them placed at Ralston's feet, but out of sight from the door, and safe from flying bullets. The lamps, casting a flickering light on Ralston's face, made him appear eerie. Jonas and the others, all ten of them, entered and walked by the councilman, continuing out the back of the house without a word. They nodded grimly at Stryker as they passed.

Cavin entered last, carrying a shotgun. He had four more men behind him, each with a shotgun. "Met up outside, Jonas told us what to do. If that bunch wants to get rough, we'll put holes in 'em." He said, patting the two-barrel. "'Bout time we stop actin' like fuckin' sheep getting' sheered." The rancher and his men went on through the house, and out the back.

The front door remained open. Stryker didn't close it. Ralston sat and stared grimly into the night. Stryker told him what to say when the Los Angeles gunman showed. He was thinking it wouldn't go well.

They arrived on foot. Silently, twenty-three men surrounded the house. All wore suits and ties and carried shotguns with handguns holstered outside the suits. Fifteen lined up on the street in front, eight stationed themselves behind the house. The men held the shotguns, stocks jammed against their hips, barrels pointed upward, confidant they outnumbered and outgunned those gathered inside. The men in front spread along a straight line in front of the house.

"Ralston!" A gunman in the center of the line yelled. "That you?"

The councilman straightened in his chair. The leather straps had shrunk enough to cut into his wrists. His face and head ached from Libra's beating. "Yes, it's me." The weak reply reflected his condition.

"Tell 'em," Stryker growled. He lay on the floor under the front window. Libra crouched next to him. Elfego lay in the hallway facing the kitchen.

"I told these folks in here you're gonna take their water," Ralston croaked out to them.

"Say it again! Louder!" Stryker ordered.

"I told 'em you're gonna steal their water!" Ralston shouted. "Those irrigation ditches are for use doing it! That you'll take all the water! Told 'em Werner and Books are liars! Don't trust . . ."

Three shotgun blasts tore into Ralston's body, two in his chest, one in his face, turning it into a crimson mask. A cacophony of shotguns then exploded, sending hundreds of pellets through the door and the two windows, shattering the glass, shredding the curtains. A second set of shotguns erupted from the eight men stationed in back of the house. The blasts entered the kitchen through the door and windows.

The firing paused. Libra peered over the window's ledge.

"Get down!" Stryker gripped her arm and pulled hard. But a .44 round drilled into her left eye, blowing a chunk of skull and brains out the back of her head. She hit the floor beside him as a corpse. Gunmen front and rear fired handguns in rapid fire. Bullets peppered the walls inside the house, knocking off wall pictures, smashing vases. Then, there was a lull in the firing as they reloaded their revolvers.

Suddenly another set of shotgun blasts erupted behind the gunmen, coming from the dry creek-bed. Cavin and the rest had opened fire right on cue. Eight L.A. gunmen took pellets in the backs of their suits, and they crashed to the ground. Then Winchesters firing from the creek-bed dropped another four. At first, the surprised gunmen had no idea where the shots came from. It took a few seconds before they realized the shots came not from the house but from the rear. One gunman turned and yelled a warning before a 30-30 slug felled him. The remaining three dazed, but still standing, scattered. Two trailed blood.

The eight men in back, not aware of what had happened in front, waited, holding fire until the shooting stopped in front. They rushed the door and were greeted by a blast from Baca's shotgun. Elfego dropped the shotgun and fired the Winchester. He worked the lever rapidly, sending four more rounds through the door. The blast from the double-barreled twelve-gauge blew the first two men back outside. A 30-30 slug smashed into the forehead of a third. The remaining five men retreaded to the cover of the cottonwood tree and considered their options. After a short while, one man was elected to run around the house and find out how the attack was going. He returned shortly with the bad news. The five men faded into the night.

Jonas and the others in the creek bed did as Stryker told them. Cavin had spread his men out, placing them between every one or two town folk. Jonas had no problem letting the war-hardened rancher take charge. The old infantry sergeant walked the line, checking weapons and firing positions. His military competence bolstered confidence, shored up courage. Once they'd fired the shotguns and exactly four rounds from the Winchesters, they bent low and ran down the gully, away from the house and town. Not one of them was injured. Circling back, they eventually worked their way to the rear entrance of the Laws Hardware store.

Stryker slowly got to his feet, having waited a good five minutes after the shooting stopped. He had yet to fire a single shot.

"Baca!"

"Here! They gone?" Came the reply from the kitchen.

"Yeah."

Elfego came down the hall to the living room. "Ah damn." He saw Libra's body lying in a pool of blood on the floor.

Libra had become the second person Stryker had recently met whose life has made an unpredictable contribution. First there was Albert and now Libra. Stryker never expected her to help him save Owens Valley water. Stryker couldn't know about Albert's impact nearly a century later, he did witness Libra's. *You just never know*, he thought.

Stryker crouched low and in one quick move, stepped through the door to get outside the house. Bodies lay strewn in in a ragged line on the street, visible in the bluish light of a full moon. Curious town folk apparently held their curiosity in check. No one had yet to venture out to see the carnage in front of Libra's home. Stryker dropped off the porch. He crept to each corner and inspected both sides of the house. Seeing no one, he turned his attention to the street. He started at the first body on the right and checked for survivors. When he found one moaning, he put a .44 in his head. The single shot sounded loud. Another wounded survivor three bodies away crawled, slowly and silently. Obviously in pain, yet he was desperate to escape a bullet. A second shot reverberated in the night, ending his short journey.

"I think four or five escaped in back," Elfego said, walking up. "These all dead now?"

"Saw two or three running toward town." Stryker kicked his boot against the last man's face.

"What now, Stryker?"

"Bishop Creek."

"Well, I'll go make arrangements for Libra and go see about the kid," Baca said, scanning the street toward Laws. "The suits from Los Angeles have probably had enough, but I'll go to Bishop with ya if you need me."

"No need."

____

CHAPTER THIRTEEN

____

Baca came upon the undertaker in front of Laws Hardware and interrupted Jonas who was describing the large burial job to the elderly mortician. The rest of the volunteers remained inside the store, nervously telling each other how lucky they were. They passed around a bottle, each one taking big swallows of the rye whiskey.

"Still, don't seem right." Rolf took a swig and passed the bottle. "Shooting 'em in the back."

"Them men were trying to kill everybody in the house," Angel answered, grabbing the bottle. "And he tolt us to wait til they started shootin'. If we'd a been in there they'd a kilt us. Come in and shot us all."

"Where is Stryker anyway?" Sophie asked.

"My guess, he's gone to cut off a snake's head." Angel passed the bottle.

Outside the door, another conversation took place.

"Before you tend to them other fellows, Alfred" Baca said. "Take care of the Libra woman inside the house. And don't pile her on your wagon with 'em other fuckers. Treat her different and treat her special. I'll be back in the mornin'."

"They kill Libra?" Jonas asked.

"Yeah, make sure he . . ." Baca dipped his head sideways at Alfred. "Fixes her up right." He stepped from the boardwalk onto the street and turned back to the two men. "They killed Cleo too. God damn them," Baca said angrily.

Jonas stepped to the edge of the boardwalk and yelled, "Where you going now, Gunner?"

"Gett'n my fuckin' horse."

Riding to the Righteous Sisters' camp, Elfego maintained his foul mood. It got worse when he got closer and heard gunfire. He spurred the horse to an all-out gallop. Rabbit holes be damned.

Four men stood abreast, twenty feet from the wagon, firing their six-shooters, pouring lead in the canvas. An occasional shot was coming from the wagon, with no effect. Carbine in one hand, the Colt in the other, Elfego charged. He rode right through them. A 30-30 slug dropped one; three rounds from the revolver felled two more. He wheeled his mount for another charge. Somehow the animal stayed upright. The last man took off running. Elfego booted the Winchester and flipped the Colt to his right hand. He caught the fleeing man and fired two bullets in his back.

Baca rode back to the wagon. "Shane!" He leapt to the ground.

"In here–Gunner?" He forgot it wasn't the right name.

"Yeah, it's me. Ya all right, kid?"

Shane poked his head out, peeking from the rear of the Conestoga. "Yeah." Shane jumped to the ground to meet Baca running to the back of the wagon. "They tried to steal the mules. I shot one. I think they killed them women in there." He stuck his boot on a wheel spoke and peered over the wagon gate. "Eula?"

"Eula's dead. So's Hany." Jemima muttered.

"You hurt?" Shane asked.

"No, I'm all right." Jemima, shaking badly, was nowhere near the grieving stage yet. She climbed over her sisters' bodies, and Shane helped her to the ground. The two hugged briefly and broke apart. Jemima put her arm around Shane's shoulders and held him close beside her, facing Baca. Apparently, too upset to think clearly, they stood and waited for Baca to tell them what to do.

"All right, gather up what you can, and you two drive in the wagon behind me to Libra's house." Baca left out her fate for the time being. Maybe by the time they got to town, Alfred will have cleaned up outside, meaning Libra's body would be gone too. Elfego didn't want to see her body again.

Stryker rode into Bishop Creek from the north. He had no idea what Werner looked like, or the engineer with him. He suspected they'd be at the Bishop Creek Hotel though, staying away from the dirty work. They kept their hands clean and stayed clear of gunfire. Cowards. If he ran into the clerk, he'd remember him. Didn't matter. He was there to kill 'em. Anyone else who got in his way would get a bullet too. Stryker was in a bad mood.

The door to room four was open. Werner waited eagerly for the news from Laws. Stryker entered.

Werner sat on a bed across the room, one black boot rested on a table with boot polish, cup of water, and cotton balls. He held the other boot, applying a high gloss on its toe with a wet cotton ball. "Can I help you, Sir?" The commissioner stopped buffing. A nervous smile crossed his face.

"Werner." Stryker said.

The commissioner nodded.

Stryker came closer. He eyed the items on the table. "Stuff the cotton in your ears."

"My ears?" Werner's smile disappeared. "Why?"

"Screams."

"Screams, what screams?" Werner looked frightened now.

"Yours." Stryker fisted the sai from his back.

Stryker had to smash open door five with his boot. Cole Books hovered over a topographical map spread on the table. The cries from room four hadn't been loud enough to alert him there was trouble. He turned and straightened. Backing up, he tripped and fell on the bed. Stryker sprang on him, straddling his chest. Books' mouth flew open in protest. The long tine of the sai slid past the words in his throat.

Stryker sat aboard the eight o'clock train leaving Laws the next morning. The train whistle blew as the hotel maid opened the door to room four. She let out a loud screech heard throughout the hotel. But Werner didn't hear it. He wouldn't have heard, even without cotton in his ears.

The only man from Los Angeles to survive–the two wounded suits succumbed to their wounds before dawn–sat in a rail car behind Stryker's. He hadn't recognized Stryker, nor Stryker him. No matter, his part in the water wars had ended. Upon returning to southern California, he planned to slip quietly back to work as a night watchman, and he won't make *no fucking report to nobody.*

Stryker hadn't sought out Baca or the kid prior to leaving, and he failed to learn of Eula's and Hany's fate before he got on the train. His job was finished. Once the action began, it ended quickly, and the rest did not concern him.

When Stryker arrived in San Francisco, he stabled the roan and took the cable car on Montgomery Street to the Palace Hotel. Returning to San Francisco still affected him in a positive way because it's where he grew up. And now Morgan lived there. However, he could no longer live in the city. Out under the wide-open skies of the west is where he belonged, and San Francisco wasn't part of that. No oceans, boats, or salt-water fish, lay on the trail between the roan's ears. So even though the city stirred something inside him, it wasn't a longing to live there.

The hotel attaché came back quickly. Stryker was to come right up to the senator's suite.

"Stryker!" George Hearst opened the door to his suite himself. "Come in! Want a drink, coffee? You hungry?"

"No."

"Come sit." Hearst directed Stryker to take a seat in one of the wing-back chairs by the window. The senator sensed Stryker intended the meeting be brief when he refused the offer of food and drink. But Hearst wanted the man to be planted long enough for him to hear a complete accounting of events in Bishop Creek. "Didn't hear from the woman who asked for help," Hearst said as he poured himself a glass of whiskey. "I got a telegram, though. Said there was quite a ruckus over there. The commissioner from Los Angeles got killed, his chief engineer too. And then there was a group of citizens from Southern California got all shot." Hearst left it open for a response. No direct questions or accusations to a man who slits throats as a salutation.

"The woman who sent for your help is dead. The bunch from Los Angeles murdered her and several more. The folks there figured out the commissioner from L.A. and his gang came to steal their water, and would kill whoever tried to stop 'em. The locals formed a group to fight back. When the commissioner's men tried to kill everyone in a meeting two nights ago, they got ambushed. Werner, the commissioner, and his engineer, got killed same night."

"So, they kept their water," Hearst said.

"Yes."

"They'll try again someday. Los Angeles is a thirsty town."

Indeed, they did a couple decades later, and they got the water. And that is how Owens Lake became the largest single source of dust pollution in the United States.

Hearst rose quickly to his feet, but Stryker had gotten up first. "Thanks, Stryker." Hearst knew better than to offer his hand. "Your regular room is ready for you."

Stryker turned and walked out the door. Hearst hadn't said if he knew Gunner to actually be Baca. The Senator had contacts. He probably did, Stryker thought. No matter. The room Hearst arranged for him lay one floor down from the Senator's top floor, and he needed a bath.

He'd been soaking in the bathtub for ten minutes when the door swung open. Left unlocked, Stryker expected a visitor, a very pretty one. Morgan walked in, marched over to the bathtub. Classic profile, high cheekbones, sharp facial lines, dark hair parted on the side, shoulder length, Morgan wore an open-collared white shirt and khaki slacks. Legs splayed, hands on hips, she said, "Hello Stryker."

Damn, she looked good. He'd never met a woman like this one. They stood on equal ground, him and her. Fair trade. Neither had an advantage, nor did they try for one. Intelligent and good-looking, trim and athletic, she was a hell of a woman. She stood by the tub with a twinkle in her eye. Under the soap suds, about halfway down, a part of him stirred.

"Shall I join you?" Morgan unbuttoned her shirt. She sat on the chair by the tub to pull off her boots, after that the rest came off quickly. Stepping into the tub, she lowered herself, pushing her back against his chest. She could feel his manhood on her spine.

Natural, that's how she felt. He wrapped his arms around her, pulling Morgan even closer.

She snuggled against him, leaning her head to one side, exposing a delicate neck for a kiss. She got it. She got several up and down her neck, sending little tingles down past her stomach. When his hands cup her breasts and he began gently pinching her nipples, she knew the bath wouldn't last much longer. "Let's not get the bed wet," she said. She lifted herself from the soapy water and stepped from the tub. No towels were within reach and she sank to the rug on the floor. Morgan paused a moment and got to all fours. That's when she looked at Stryker with arched eyebrows and a smile. "Well?"

Stryker got out of the tub, splashing water. Positioning himself behind Morgan, he entered her in one long hard stroke, eliciting a loud grunt from the woman. Grabbing her hips, Stryker began a series of regular, but urgent stroking. Morgan pushed back with each thrust, causing her hair to fly up in short jerky flips. Her little grunts kept pace with the strokes, and she bobbed her head, tossing her hair–like a horse with his mane.

Stryker paused, leaving only the tip inside her. Poised to ram in again, he gripped Morgan's hip, digging his fingers into the soft skin of her buttocks. "Bark."

"What?" Morgan pushed, attempting to pull him back into her.

"Bark, like a dog," Stryker ordered.

"I'm not gonna do that," she laughed.

He pulled out completely. "Bark."

She tried to get him inside again, but he stayed away. "You fucker."

"Do it."

"Woof." It was just a little bark.

"Again, louder."

Morgan looked back at Stryker with a mischievous smile. "Woof," and laughed again.

Now, there are a lot of men who live dull, unimaginative lives. They hunch over their desks, or toil in other monotonous jobs all day long. They have no sense of adventure, no imagination, and have sex only to reproduce. They adhere to biblical guidance with guilty pleasure. And all are married to unhappy wives. To those men that little "woof" would have gone unnoticed.

Stryker is not one. He rammed and exploded.

Morgan later said it felt like a firehose.

She rolled on her back and they continued on and off for another hour.

"I know you won't be staying. Where do you go when you leave?" Morgan asked. She lay with Stryker, her head on his chest, her hand carelessly caressing his flat stomach.

"Pescadero."

"You like it."

"Yes."

"I won't go there. You should have it to yourself. You can come here though."

"Yes."

✕

"You had to know Gunner–or Baca wouldn't stay, honey." Jemima said to Shane, as they watched the man ride off. They both stood and watched Baca grow smaller until they couldn't see him anymore.

Shane, the only living relative for Cleo and Libra, inherited their two properties. Baca helped them sell off the cattle. After a month, Baca had received a letter requesting his help in Texas. He owed another favor. Jemima, stayed though. Shane had grown attached to the negro woman, a mother figure maybe. He begged her to stay, live in Libra's house with him. The townspeople in Laws agreed as long as she stayed, Shane wouldn't need a guardian.

"Say, Shane, you hungry?" Jemima asked, as they stood still staring at the distant, now empty, landscape.

"I guess so."

"What d'you like this mornin'?"

"How about pancakes?"

INTERVIEW WITH FIRST COMICS NEWS

by Tim Chizmar

Every so often, in my line of work, I run across TALENT. Pure, complete and utter writing devastation. That's what writer WES RAND has in his tales of the anti-hero EVIL STRYKER. If you've ever wondered what the Punisher would look like in the Wild West or perhaps how fighting, drinking, sexing and an ounce of morality would play out… you've met your storyteller!

HERE IS MY CHAT WITH WES:

1) Have you always wanted to be a writer?

No, I had been reading a western series which ended, and I got tired of good guys taking bad guys in to stand trial. I wanted a character who is so damn mean, the bad guys are afraid of him.

2) What works inspired you to pursue this career?
 Edge Series by George Gilman

3) Do you have an ideal reader in mind?
 Yes, educated professionals, readers who relate to a conservative philosophy, readers who want quick justice, not the traditional purple sage western reader, and women who like men with balls.

4) Why do you choose the words you do?
 I try to imagine the characters talking and acting, saying and doing things which fit their personas. I like simple, yet descriptive, prose. I want the stories to be easy to read, no fuzziness, clean and bold.

5) Who would play your characters in a movie?
 Jack Palance for Stryker, Dagny Taggart (ok maybe Angelina Jolie) for Morgan.

6) What are the biggest mistakes new writers make?
 Thinking that their shit is great and writing is easy.

7) Have you been to comic-con?
 No

8) What is success to you?
 To be widely read, affecting reader's philosophical perspectives, so that they realize socialism sucks.

9) How does politics factor into your narrative?
 See question 8 answer

10) Advice for wannabe writers who haven't committed yet?
 Write. Write what you like. Write what you'd enjoy reading. If you do, you'll be more likely to write regularly. Let others correct your grammar, you tell the story you would want to read, to feel.

***

About Tim Chizmar

When TIM CHIZMAR was a child he lost himself in evil, scary books. One day a morally righteous librarian refused to let him take out his books. Reading about demons, be-headings, and cannibalism wasn't the norm in Linesville, Pennsylvania. When Tim brought his mother there, she insisted that her son be allowed to read WHATEVER HE WANTED. This upset the librarian so she looked his mother in the eye and said, "Your son is gonna grow up to be a great horror writer one day.. OR A SERIAL KILLER." As of this writing, Tim hasn't killed anyone.. YET.. but he has wrote and sold many screenplays in Hollywood. When he's not burying bodies.. Tim is a comedian, actor, director, and producer living in Los Angeles, CA. He is the Director, Producer, and co-writer of NAKED ALIEN MASSACRE. What drives Tim's success is knowing that somewhere in Pennsylvania a librarian is praying for his soul.

ACKNOWLEDGMENTS

Thanks to Tim Chizmar, my energizer publicist, Stacey Smekofske, the most excellent editor a writer can have.

Also, special thanks to Diane Kawasaki, Writer and star of TLC's hit show MY LITTLE LIFE for her support and kind words.

And lastly, thanks to my wonderful children, Anna and Tyler, and Tom, my son n law and good friend.

Wes Rand was an Artillery Officer in the U.S. Army during the 1960's. He pays alimony. He doesn't like to golf but lives on a golf course. He has been bucked off a horse and two women.

He has a cabin in the mountains where he writes and hikes while his wife plays golf in Las Vegas. Wes enjoys living under the open skies in Nevada and Utah.

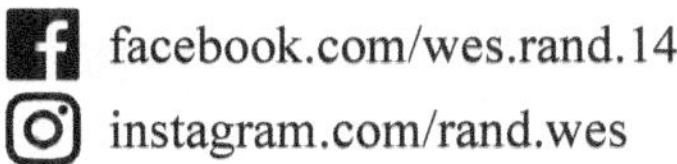